PDCCI

Mystery

14⁹⁵

HE CRAWLED ON HANDS AND KNEES.

The Missing Chums.   *Frontispiece* (*Page* 144)

THE HARDY BOYS
THE
MISSING CHUMS

By
FRANKLIN W. DIXON
AUTHOR OF
THE HARDY BOYS: THE TOWER TREASURE
THE HARDY BOYS: THE SECRET OF THE OLD MILL

ILLUSTRATED BY
WALTER S. ROGERS

FACSIMILE EDITION

BEDFORD, MA
APPLEWOOD BOOKS

For further information about these editions, please write:
Applewood Books, P.O. Box 365, Bedford, MA 01730.

LIBRARY OF CONGRESS CATALOGING-IN-PUBLICATION DATA
Dixon, Franklin W.
    The missing chums / by Franklin W. Dixon; illustrated by Walter S. Rogers.—Facsimile ed.
    p.   cm.
    Summary: When the Hardy Boys set out to solve the mystery of their missing chums, they discover a gang hide-out in a cave on an island along the way.
    ISBN 1-55709-147-1
    [1. Missing persons—Fiction.   2. Mystery and detective stories.]   I. Rogers, Walter S., ill.   II. Title.
PZ7.D644Mi   1996
[Fic]–dc20   96-7469
                                          CIP
                                          AC

10 9 8 7 6 5 4 3 2

PUBLISHER'S NOTE

Much has changed in America since the Hardy Boys series first began in 1927. The modern reader may be delighted with the warmth and exactness of the language, the wholesome innocence of the characters, their engagement with the natural world, or the nonstop action without the use of violence; but just as well, the modern reader may be extremely uncomfortable with the racial and social stereotyping, the roles women play in these books, or the use of phrases or situations which may conjure up some response in the modern reader that was not felt by the reader of the times.

For good or bad, we Americans have changed quite a bit since these books were first issued. Many readers will remember these editions with great affection and will be delighted with their return; others will wonder why we just don't let them disappear. These books are part of our heritage. They are a window on our real past. For that reason, except for the addition of this note, we are presenting *The Missing Chums* unedited and unchanged from its first edition.

Applewood Books

THE HARDY BOYS

THE MISSING CHUMS

By
FRANKLIN W. DIXON

AUTHOR OF

THE HARDY BOYS: THE TOWER TREASURE
THE HARDY BOYS: THE SECRET OF THE OLD MILL

ILLUSTRATED BY
WALTER S. ROGERS

NEW YORK
GROSSET & DUNLAP
PUBLISHERS

Made in the United States of America

MYSTERY STORIES FOR BOYS

By FRANKLIN W. DIXON

THE HARDY BOYS: THE TOWER TREASURE

THE HARDY BOYS: THE HOUSE ON THE CLIFF

THE HARDY BOYS: THE SECRET OF THE OLD MILL

THE HARDY BOYS: THE MISSING CHUMS

THE HARDY BOYS: HUNTING FOR HIDDEN GOLD

GROSSET & DUNLAP, PUBLISHERS, NEW YORK

The Hardy Boys: The Missing Chums

CONTENTS

iv   Contents

THE HARDY BOYS:
THE MISSING CHUMS

CHAPTER I

THE THREE STRANGERS

"You certainly ought to have a dandy trip."

"I'll say we will, Frank! We sure wish you could come along."

Frank Hardy grinned ruefully and shook his head.

"I'm afraid we're out of luck. Joe and I may take a little trip later on, but we can't make it this time."

"Just think of it!" said Chet Morton, the other speaker. "A whole week motorboating along the coast! We're the lucky boys, eh, Biff?"

Biff Hooper, at the wheel of his father's new motorboat, nodded emphatically.

"You bet we're lucky. I'm glad dad got this boat in time for the summer holidays. I've been dreaming of a trip like that for years."

"It won't be the same without the Hardy

1

Boys," returned Chet. "I had it all planned out that Frank and Joe would be coming along with us in their own boat and we'd make a real party of it."

"Can't be done," observed Joe Hardy, settling himself more comfortably in the back of the boat. "There's nothing Frank and I would like better—but duty calls!" he exclaimed dramatically, slapping himself on the chest.

"Duty, my neck!" grunted Frank. "We just have to stay at home while dad is in Chicago, that's all. It'll be pretty dull without Chet and Biff around to help us kill time."

"You can put in the hours thinking of Biff and me," consoled Chet. "At night you can just picture us sitting around our campfire away up the coast, and in the daytime you can imagine us speeding away out over the bounding main." He postured with one foot on the gunwale. "A sailor's life for me, my hearties! Yo, ho, and a bottle of ink!"

The boat gave a sudden lurch at that moment, for Biff Hooper had not yet mastered the art of navigation and Chet wavered precariously for a few seconds, finally losing his balance and sitting down heavily in a smear of grease at the bottom of the craft.

> *"Yo ho, and a bottle of ink*
> *And he nearly fell into the drink,"*

chanted Frank Hardy, as the boys roared with laughter at their chum's discomfiture.

"Poet!" sniffed Chet, as he got up. Then, as he gingerly felt the seat of his trousers: "Another pair of pants ready for the cleaners. I ought to wear overalls when I go boating." He grinned as he said it, for Chet Morton was the soul of good nature and it took a great deal more than a smear of grease to erase his ready smile.

The four boys, Frank and Joe Hardy, Chet Morton and Biff Hooper, all chums in the same set at the Bayport high school, were out on Barmet Bay in the *Envoy,* the Hooper motorboat, helping Biff learn to run the craft. Their assistance consisted chiefly of mocking criticisms of the luckless Biff's posture at the helm and sundry false alarms to the effect that the boat was springing a leak or that the engine was about to blow up. Each announcement had the effect of precipitating the steersman into a panic of apprehension and sending his tormentors into convulsions of laughter.

Biff had made good progress, however, as he had been with the Hardy boys on previous occasions in their own motorboat, the *Sleuth,* and he had picked up the rudiments of handling the craft. He was anxious to be a first-rate pilot before starting up the coast on his projected trip with Chet Morton the following week. He had an aptitude for mechanics and he was satisfied that he would have a thorough understanding of his boat by the time they were ready to start.

"If the coast guards find two little boys like you roaming around in a great big motorboat they're likely to give you a spanking and send you back home," laughed Frank. "I'll bet you'll be back in Bayport inside of two days."

"Rats!" replied Chet, inelegantly, if forcefully. "If our grub holds out we'll be away more than the week."

"There's no danger of that. Not with you along," Joe remarked, and deftly dodged a wad of waste that Chet flung at him. Chet Morton's enormous appetite was proverbial among the chums.

"Just sore because you can't come along with us," Chet scoffed. "You know mighty well that the two of you would give your eye-teeth to be on this trip. Oh, well, we'll tell you all about it when we get back."

"A lot of comfort that will be!"

"A leak!" roared Chet suddenly, pounding Biff on the back. "The boat has sprung a leak. Get a pail!"

"What!" shouted Biff, in alarm, starting up from the wheel. Then, for the fifth time that afternoon, he realized that he had been fooled and he sank back with a look of disgust on his face.

"Some time that boat *will* spring a leak and I won't believe you," he warned, settling down to his steering again.

"I'll be good," promised Chet, sitting down and looking out over the bay. "Say, there's a big brute of a motorboat coming along behind us, isn't it?"

"I'll say she's big," Frank agreed, looking back. "I don't remember ever having seen that boat around here before."

"Me neither," declared Joe. "I wonder where it came from."

The strange craft was painted a dingy gray. It was large and unwieldy and did not ride easily in the water. Although that boat was some distance in the wake of their own craft the boys could distinguish the figures of three men, all seated well up toward the front. Biff glanced back.

"It's a new one on me," he said. "I've never seen it before."

"Sure has lots of power, anyway," Chet commented. The roar of the engine could be plainly heard across the water. In spite of its clumsy appearance, the big boat ploughed ahead at good speed, and, as Bill had the *Envoy,* his craft, throttled down, the second boat was slowly overtaking them.

"Let's wait till they get abreast of us and give them a race," Chet suggested.

"Not on your life," objected Biff. "I'm only learning to run this tub and I'm not in the racing class yet. Besides, there are too many other boats out in the bay this afternoon. I'd be sure to run into one of them."

The boys watched as the other craft overtook them. The big motorboat ploughed noisily ahead, keeping directly in their wake.

"I wonder if the man at the helm is asleep," said Frank. "He doesn't seem to be making any attempt to pull over."

"He's awake, all right," declared Chet. "I can see him talking to the man beside him. He won't run us down. Don't worry—not with Captain Hooper at the helm, my hearties!"

The roaring of the pursuing craft suddenly took on a new note and the big boat seemed to leap out of the water as it increased its speed and bore rapidly down on the *Envoy*. Spray flew about the heads of the helmsman and his two passengers and a high crest of foam rose from either side of the bow. Biff Hooper shifted the wheel slightly and the *Envoy* veered in toward the shore. To the surprise of the boys, the other boat also changed its course and continued directly in their wake.

"The idiots!" exclaimed Biff.

"I don't get the idea of this at all," muttered Frank Hardy to his brother. "What are they following us so closely for?"

Joe shrugged. "Probably just trying to give us a scare."

The other boat was now almost upon their craft. It nosed out to the right and drew alongside, coming dangerously close. The boys could see the three men clearly and they noticed that all three scrutinized them, seeming to pay particular attention to Chet and Biff.

The men were unsavory looking fellows, unshaven, surly of expression. The man at the helm was sharp-featured and keen-eyed, while the other two were of heavier build. One of the pair wore a cap, while the other man was bare-headed, revealing a scant thatch of carroty hair so close-cropped that it seemed to stick out at all angles to his cranium. This man, the boys saw, nudged his companion and pointed to Biff, who was too busy at the helm of his own craft to notice.

"Not so close!" yelled Chet, seeing that the other boat was running broadside in dangerous proximity to the *Envoy*.

In reply, the man at the helm of the other craft merely sneered and brought his boat in until the two speeding launches were almost touching sides.

"What's the idea?" Joe shouted. "Trying to run us down?"

Biff Hooper shifted the wheel so that the *Envoy* would edge away from the other boat, and in this effort he was successful, for a gap of water was soon apparent between the speeding craft. But in escaping one danger he had risked another.

Two sailboats that had been flitting about Barmet Bay that afternoon were racing with the wind, and they now came threshing along with billowing canvas, immediately into the course of the motorboat. Biff had seen the sailboats previously and had judged his own course accordingly, but in his efforts to get away from the mysterious launch he had unwittingly maneuvered the *Envoy* into such a position that a collision now seemed inevitable.

The sailboats seemed to loom right up before him, not more than a hundred yards away. They were racing close together, one boat but a nose in the lead. They were scudding along with the wind at high speed and the motorboat roared down upon them.

Biff Hooper bent desperately over the helm. He was so close that no matter which way he turned it seemed impossible that he could miss one or the other of the sailboats. If he turned to the right he would crash into them head-on; if he turned to the left he would run before them and a general smash-up might be the result.

The men in the sailboats were also aware of their danger.

The boys had a glimpse of one man waving his arms. One of the boats veered out abruptly and the yardarm swung around. The sailboat was lying directly in the path of the *Envoy*.

The roaring of the engine, the threshing of the sails, the warning shouts of the boys, all created a confusion of sound. The white sails seemed to loom high above the speeding boat. A hideous collision appeared to be inevitable.

CHAPTER II

QUICK THINKING

EVERY second was precious.

Frank Hardy realized the full extent of their peril and in the same moment he realized the only way of averting it.

Without a word he sprang toward the helm, brushing Biff Hooper aside. In this emergency, Biff was helpless. Swiftly, Frank bore down on the wheel, bringing the boat around into the wind. At the same time, he opened up the throttle so that the *Envoy* leaped forward at her highest speed.

The motorboat passed just a few inches in front of the bow of the first sailboat; so close, Chet Morton said afterward, that he "could count every stitch on the patch in the sailcloth." But the danger was not yet over. There was still the other sailboat to be considered. It was pounding along immediately ahead of them; the man at the tiller was making frantic efforts to get out of the way, but the danger lay in the fact that in trying to guess the pos-

sible course of the *Envoy* he might make a
false move that would have him shoot directly
across its path.

Frank swung the helm around again. Once
more, the *Envoy* veered to the left so sharply
that a cloud of spray drenched the boys. Another shift of the wheel and the motorboat zig-
zagged safely past the sailboat and on out into
open water.

Not one of the boys had uttered a word during this. They had been tense and anxious,
but now that the peril of a smash-up had been
averted, they sank back with sighs of relief.

"I sure thought we were headed for Davy
Jones' locker that time!" breathed Chet.

Biff Hooper looked up at Frank.

"Thanks," he said. "I'd have never got out
of that mess if you hadn't taken the wheel. I
was so rattled that I didn't know what to do."

"After you've run the boat a few more weeks
you'll get so used to it that it'll be second nature to you. But that sure was a tight
squeeze," Frank admitted. "It mighty near
meant that you wouldn't have had any motorboat left to go on that trip with."

"It mighty near meant that we wouldn't
have been left to make the trip at all," Chet
declared solemnly. "What say we go home?
I've had enough excitement for one day."

"It's beginning to rain, anyway," Biff remarked, glancing up at the sky. "I guess we may as well go back."

The sky had clouded over in the past hour and the eastern sky was black, while scurrying masses of ragged clouds flew overhead before the stiffening wind. A few drops of water splashed into the boat, then came a gust of rain, followed by a light shower that passed over in a few minutes. The big motorboat that had crowded them had disappeared.

"A real storm coming up," Frank said. "Let's make for the boathouse."

The *Envoy* headed for Bayport.

"I'd like to tell those three fellows in that other boat what I think of them," declared Biff. "They got us into that jam. They were crowding me so close that I didn't have a chance to keep an eye on the sailboats."

"I still can't see why they drew up alongside," Joe observed. "They seemed mighty inquisitive. Gave us all the once-over."

Chet offered a solution.

"Perhaps they thought we were some one else and when they found out their mistake they went away."

"But they *didn't* go away," Frank pointed out. "They kept crowding us over. And one of them pointed at Biff."

"At me?"

"Yes."

"I didn't notice that."

"He seemed to recognize you and was pointing you out to the other men."

"Well, if he recognized me I can't return the compliment. I never saw any of them before in my life."

"He was probably pointing you out as a unique specimen," ventured Joe, with a grin. "Probably those fellows are from a museum, Biff. They'll likely make an offer for your carcass after you're dead and they'll have it stuffed and put it on display in a glass case. That's why they were so interested."

Joe's suggestion elicited warm words from Biff and a friendly struggle ensued. Inasmuch as Biff Hooper was the champion boxer and wrestler of Bayport High, Joe was at a disadvantage, and paid for his derogatory remarks by being held over the side by the scruff of the neck and given a ducking until he pleaded for mercy.

By the time the boys reached Bayport it was raining heavily, and after leaving the *Envoy* in the boathouse they raced up the street to the Hardy boys' home. The barn in the back yard was a favorite retreat of the chums and there they spent many of their Saturday afternoons. The barn was fitted up as a gymnasium, with parallel bars, a trapeze, boxing gloves and a punching bag, and was an ideal refuge on a rainy day. The thrilling experience with the sailboats and the mystery of the strange motorboat were soon forgotten.

Phil Cohen and Tony Prito, school chums of the Hardy boys, drifted in during the afternoon, as well as Jerry Gilroy and "Slim" Robinson. This comprised the "gang," of which the two Hardy boys were the leading spirits.

Frank and Joe Hardy were the sons of Fenton Hardy, an internationally famous detective. Mr. Hardy had been for many years a detective on the New York police force, where he was so successful that he went into practice for himself. His two sons already showed signs of inheriting his ability and in a number of instances had solved difficult criminal cases.

The first of these was the mystery of the theft of valuable jewels and bonds from Tower Mansion, an old-fashioned building on the outskirts of Bayport. How the Hardy boys solved the mystery has already been related in the first volume of this series, entitled, "The Tower Treasure."

In the second volume, "The House on the Cliff," the Hardy boys and their chums had a thrilling experience in a reputedly haunted house on the cliffs overlooking Barmet Bay. This was the starting point of an exciting chase for smugglers, in which the Hardy boys came to the rescue of their father after undergoing many dangers in the cliff caves.

The third volume of the series, "The Mystery of the Old Mill," which precedes the present book, relates the efforts of the Hardy boys to run to earth a gang of counterfeiters operating in and about Bayport and their efforts to solve the mystery surrounding an abandoned mill in the farming country back of Barmet Bay.

Frank Hardy, a tall, dark-haired boy of sixteen, was a year older than his brother Joe, and usually took the lead in their exploits, although Joe was not a whit behind his brother in shrewdness and in deductive ability.

Mrs. Hardy viewed their passion for detective work with considerable apprehension, preferring that they plan to go to a university and direct their energies toward entering one of the professions; but the success of the lads had been so marked in the cases on which they had been engaged that she had by now almost resigned herself to seeing them destined for careers as private detectives when they should grow older.

Just now, however, detective work was farthest from their thoughts. Frank and Tony Prito were engaged in some complicated maneuvers on the parallel bars, Joe was taking a boxing lesson from Biff Hooper, and Phil

Cohen was trying to learn how to walk on his hands, under the guidance of Jerry Gilroy and Slim Robinson.

As for Chet Morton, the mischief-maker, he was sitting on the window-sill, meditating. And when Chet Morton meditated, it usually meant that a practical joke was in the offing.

"I'll bet you can't 'skin the cat' on that trapeze, Jerry," he called out suddenly.

Jerry Gilroy looked up.

"Skin the cat?" he said. "Of course I can."

"Bet you can't."

"Bet I can."

"Can't."

"Can."

"Do it, then."

"Watch me."

As every boy knows, "skinning the cat" is an acrobatic feat that does not necessarily embrace cruelty to animals. Jerry Gilroy was not unjustly proud of his prowess on the trapeze and Chet Morton's doubt of his ability to perform one of the simplest stunts in his repertoire made him resolve to "skin the cat" as slowly and elaborately as lay within his power.

He grasped the trapeze bar with both hands, then swung forward, raising his feet from the floor, bending his knees. Chet edged forward, presumably to get a better view of proceedings, but at the same time he tightened his grip on a long, flat stick that he had found by the window ledge.

Jerry slowly doubled up until his feet were above his head, immediately below the bar, and then commenced the second stage of the elaborate back somersault, coming down slowly toward the floor. At this juncture the rear of his trousers was presented as a tempting mark to the waiting Chet. This was the stage of the feat for which the joker had been waiting and he raised the flat stick, bringing it down with a resounding smack on his human target.

There was a yelp of pain from Jerry and a roar of laughter from Chet. Doubled up on the bar as he was, Jerry could not immediately regain the floor, and Chet managed to belabor him twice more before the unfortunate acrobat finally found his footing. There he stood, bewildered, rubbing the seat of his trousers, with a rueful expression on his face, while Chet leaned against the wall, helpless with laughter.

The other boys joined in the merriment, for they had stopped to witness the incident, and after a while Jerry achieved a wry smile, although he looked reflectively at his tormentor as though wondering just what form his revenge should take.

No one enjoyed Chet Morton's practical jokes more than he did himself. He whooped with laughter, wiped the tears from his eyes, and leaned out of the window, spluttering with mirth.

"Oh, boy!" he giggled. "The expression— on your—face—!" Then he was away again, leaning across the window-sill weakly, shaking with laughter.

Jerry Gilroy tiptoed quietly up behind him. A quick movement and he lowered the window until it was against Chet's back.

The practical joker suddenly stopped laughing, and turned his head.

"Hey! What's the matter?" he inquired.

He was pinned down by the window and he could not see Jerry picking up the flat piece of board that had been the instrument of torture a few minutes previously. But a suspicion of the truth came to him, and a roar of laughter from the other boys warned him that vengeance was due.

It came.

Smack!

Chet Morton wriggled and squirmed, but he was pinned helplessly by the weight of the window against his shoulders, and he presented a more tempting target for Jerry's ministrations with the flat stick, and a more stationary target as well, than Jerry had presented for him.

Smack! Smack! Smack!

He roared with pain and, helpless as he was,

danced vainly on the floor in his efforts to escape. Jerry Gilroy belabored him across the rear with that stinging stick until his desire for revenge had been fully satisfied, while the other boys howled with glee at the manner in which the tables had been turned.

Finally, when Jerry tossed the flat stick away and joined the others in their laughter, Chet managed to raise the window and escape.

"Can't see what you're all laughing at," he grumbled, as he sat down carefully on a nearby box. Then he rose hurriedly and rubbed the tender spot.

"He laughs best who laughs last," quoted Jerry Gilroy.

"Guess I've got to get home," announced Biff, a moment later, and soon he and the others were on their way, dodging through the rain.

Then Frank and Joe put the barn in order and went into the house. They felt particularly carefree and never dreamed of the news they were to hear or of how it was to affect them and their chums.

CHAPTER III

A Shady Trio

"I am sure my man is in Chicago. I know for a fact that he went West, and the Windy City would naturally be his hiding place."

Fenton Hardy tapped the library table reflectively with a pencil. Mrs. Hardy put aside the magazine she had been reading.

"Are you going to follow him?"

"I'll trail him right to the Pacific Coast if necessary."

Frank and Joe Hardy, who had been standing by the window, disconsolately watching the rain streaking down the pane, looked around.

"Who is he, dad?" asked Frank.

"One of the cleverest and most daring bank robbers in the country. I've been after him for almost a year now and it's only been within the last few weeks that I've ever come anywhere near catching him."

"What's his name?"

Fenton Hardy laughed. "I've made you curious, eh? Well, this chap has about a dozen names. He has a new alias every week, but so far as the police are concerned he's known as Baldy Turk, because he's as bald as an egg. He and his gang held up a bank in a small New Jersey town about a month ago and got away with over ten thousand dollars in broad daylight. That's how I managed to get trace of him again. Even the police didn't know Baldy Turk was mixed up in the affair because he was wearing a wig that day, but he double-crossed one of the members of his gang out of his share in the loot.''

"And that fellow told the police," ventured Joe.

Mr. Hardy shook his head.

"Not the police. He didn't dare go near them because he was wanted for two or three robberies himself. But he came to me and tipped me off as to where Baldy Turk could be found. He wanted revenge. I went to New York, where Baldy was in hiding; but evidently some of his friends knew I was on his trail and he disappeared before I could lay my hands on him.''

"Where did he go then?" asked Frank, with interest.

"He hid out on Long Island for a while, but I managed to pick up the trail again and went after him, but he was too smart for me. He got away in a fast automobile and took a couple of shots at me in the bargain. I managed to get the number of the car and traced it to Manhattan and later found that Baldy Turk had left the East altogether. He bought a ticket to Cleveland, doubled back to Buffalo and managed to shake me off.''

''What makes you think he is in Chicago?''

''Because another member of his gang went to Chicago just a week ago. So I imagine Baldy Turk was to meet him there. In any case, Chicago is a thieves' paradise, so it seems logical that Baldy Turk would make for there.''

''And you're going after him! Gee, I wish I could go,'' declared Joe.

Fenton Hardy smiled.

''It's no job for a boy,'' he said. ''Baldy Turk is a bad man with a gun. If I ever do find him it will take some maneuvering to get the handcuffs on him, I'll tell you.''

''You'll be careful, won't you, Fenton,'' said Mrs. Hardy anxiously. ''I'm always frightened whenever I know you're after one of these desperate criminals.''

''I'll be as careful as I can, Laura,'' promised her husband; ''but in my business I have to take chances. Baldy Turk knows I'm after him and he doesn't mean to be caught if he can help it. He or any of the men in his gang would shoot me on sight. There's a standing reward of five thousand dollars out for Baldy and, besides, the Bankers' Association have promised me a handsome fee if I can get him behind the bars and break up the gang.''

"I won't rest easy in my mind until you're back home safe," Mrs. Hardy declared.

"Don't worry about me," replied her husband, going over to her and patting her shoulder reassuringly. "I'll get back safely all right, and Baldy Turk will be in jail if I have to chase him all over the States. The boys will look after you while I'm away."

"You bet we will!" Frank promised.

"I'm sorry it keeps you from going on that motorboat trip with Chet and Biff," Mr. Hardy remarked. "Perhaps you can arrange another jaunt after I come back."

"We're not worrying about that, dad. We don't mind staying at home."

"That's the spirit," approved their father.

"When do you leave?" Frank asked.

"I'm waiting for a letter from a friend of mine in Chicago. If he writes as I expect he will write, I should be away by the day after to-morrow."

"Then let Baldy Turk watch his step!" observed Joe.

"We'll both have to watch our step," answered Mr. Hardy, smiling. "If I don't get him, he'll probably get me."

"Well, I'm betting on you."

Mrs. Hardy shook her head doubtfully, but said nothing. She knew that her detective husband had escaped death at the hands of desperate criminals many times in the course of his career and there seemed to be no reason why he should not bring Baldy Turk to book just as he had captured many other notorious criminals in the past; but this time she had a vague premonition of danger. She knew that her husband would laugh at her fears if she expressed them, so she remained silent.

The rain had stopped, as Frank noticed when he glanced out the window again.

"It's clearing up. What say we go out for a spin, Joe?"

"Suits me."

"Let's go."

"Don't be late for supper," warned Mrs. Hardy, as the boys started out the door.

"We'll be in time," they promised, and the door closed behind them.

The Hardy boys went out to the shed where they kept their motorcycles. Both Joe and Frank had machines, given to them by their father, and in their spare time they spent many hours speeding about the roads in and around Bayport.

Their native city had a population of about fifty thousand people and was on the Atlantic coast, on Barmet Bay. There were good roads along both northern and southern arms of the bay, besides the State highway and the numerous country roads that led through the farming country back of Bayport.

Chet Morton, whose father was a real estate dealer with an office in the city, lived on a farm some distance off the road along the north arm of the bay, Chet making the daily journey to school and back in a roadster that had been given to him by his father. Chet was as proud of his roadster as the Hardy boys were proud of the motorboat that they had bought from the money they had received as reward for solving the Tower Mystery.

"Where shall we go?" asked Joe, as the Hardy boys rode out of the lane.

"Let's go to the Norton farm and see Chet."

"Good idea. I wonder if he's able to sit down yet," replied Joe, alluding to Chet's practical joke earlier in the day.

The motorcycles roared and spluttered as the boys sped along the gleaming pavements of the city. They rode through the main streets, threading their way easily through the traffic until at last they were at the outskirts of Bayport. Finally they left the city behind and reached the road leading toward the Morton farm. The leaves of the trees were still wet with rain and the luxuriant grass by the roadside glistened with the heavy drops. The air was cool and sweet after the storm. The roads had dried quickly, however, and the boys experienced no inconvenience.

They reached the Morton farmhouse in good time and Chet's sister, Iola, answered their knock. Iola was a pretty girl of about fifteen, one of the few girls at whom Joe Hardy had ever cast more than a passing glance. He lowered his eyes bashfully when she appeared in the doorway.

"Chet just left in the car about ten minutes ago," she said smilingly, in answer to their inquiry. "It's strange you didn't meet him."

"He probably went by the other road. We'll catch up to him."

"Won't you come in?"

"N-no thanks," stammered Joe, blushing. "Guess we'll be going."

"Oh, *do* come in," said Iola coaxingly. "Callie Shaw is here."

"Is she?" Frank brightened up at this intelligence, and at that moment a brown-eyed, dark-haired girl about his own age appeared in the hall.

"Hello!" she called, smiling pleasantly, and displaying small, even teeth of a dazzling whiteness.

"Let's go," muttered Joe, tugging at Frank's sleeve. He was incurably shy in the presence of girls, especially Iola.

But Frank did not go just then. He chatted with Callie Shaw for a while, and Iola tried to make conversation with Joe, whose answers were mumbled and muttered, while he inwardly wished he could talk as freely and without embarrassment as his brother. At length Frank decided to go and Joe sighed with relief. The girls bade them good-bye after again urging them to come inside the house, and the boys departed.

"Whew!" breathed Joe, mopping his brow. "I'm glad that's over."

Frank looked at him in surprise.

"Why, what's the matter? I thought you liked Iola Morton."

"That's just the trouble—I do," answered Joe mysteriously, and Frank wisely forbore further inquiry.

They mounted their motorcycles again and rode down the lane, out to the road. Hardly had they gone more than a few hundred yards, however, than Frank suddenly gestured to his brother and they slowed down.

Pulled up beside the road was an automobile, and as the boys drew near they saw that three men were in the car. The men were talking together and they looked up as the boys approached.

Something in the attitude of the trio aroused Frank's suspicions, and this prompted him to ride slower. There seemed no apparent reason why the men should have pulled their car up beside the road, for they were not repairing a breakdown and they were still a little distance from the lane leading to the Morton farmhouse. Then, as the motorcycles slowly passed the car and the three men sullenly regarded the two boys, Frank suppressed an exclamation of surprise.

The three men in the car were the three men who had pursued the boys in the motorboat earlier in the day!

Frank and Joe drove past, conscious of the scrutiny of the unsavory trio in the automobile. The men did not speak, although Frank noticed that one of them drew his cap down over his eyes and muttered something to one of his companions.

When they had gone by, Joe glanced back. The man were paying no further attention to them, but were leaning close together, evidently having resumed their interrupted conversation. There was something stealthy and secretive in their demeanor that was far from reassuring.

"Did you recognize them?" asked Frank, when they were out of earshot.

"I'll say I did! The same gang that followed us in the motorboat."

"I wonder what they're up to."

"Up to no good, by the looks of them."

"That's a queer place to park their car—so close to the Morton farm, too."

"They look like a bad outfit to me," remarked Joe.

"I'd like to know more about them. There was something funny about the way they chased us in the boat. And don't you remember how closely they looked at Chet and Biff? It seems funny to see them hanging around the farm."

"Well, they haven't done us any harm. I suppose it's none of our business—but I'd sure like to know what their game is. Let's find Chet and tell him."

They increased their speed and before long overtook Chet Morton on the shore road. But Chet laughed at their fears.

"You're too suspicious," he said. "They had probably just stopped to fix a tire when you came along. However, we'll go back to the farm and see if they're still on hand."

But when the boys drove back to the Morton farm they found that the mysterious trio in the automobile were no longer in sight.

CHAPTER IV

THE SEND-OFF

On Monday, Chet Morton and Biff Hooper set out on their motorboat trip up the coast. They were well equipped with provisions and supplies and had been up since six o'clock that morning getting the boat in readiness.

The Hardy boys went down to the dock to bid them good-bye, and although they chaffed the adventurers and laughed with them, neither Frank nor Joe could repress the disappointment they naturally felt at being unable to go with their chums.

Chet was busy stowing away the last of the provisions and Biff was tuning up the engine when the Hardy boys arrived. In a few minutes Tony Prito, at the helm of his own motorboat, arrived on the scene with Jerry Gilroy and Phil Cohen. Then, down the dock, came tripping Iola Morton and Callie Shaw.

"Hail, hail, the gang's all here!" roared Chet, when he saw them.

"Oy, what a fine day you pick for your trip!"

exclaimed Phil Cohen, looking up at the clouds. For the sky was overcast and there was no sun.

"That's all right," answered Chet. "We made up our minds to start to-day and we'd start if there was a thunderstorm on."

"Brave sailors!" mocked Callie Shaw, with a smile.

"How long will you be away?" shouted Frank.

"Until the grub runs out."

"That should be about next December," ventured Iola. "It looks to me as if you have enough provisions there to last you a year."

"Not with Chet Morton on the trip, we haven't," grunted Biff Hooper, looking up from the engine. "We'll be lucky if it lasts us a week. I've seen him eat before."

"I'll do my share," Chet promised modestly.

"We should have had the City Band down to give you a proper send-off," Joe Hardy remarked.

"It doesn't matter. We'll forgive you this time. But be sure and have the band here to welcome us when we come back."

"You'll be back by to-morrow night," declared Iola. "I know you! Why, I'll bet you'll both be scared green when darkness comes on. One night will cure you of sleeping in the open."

"Rats!" replied Chet good-naturedly. "I'm not afraid of the dark."

"Cut out the jawing and let's get started," said Biff Hooper. "No use hanging around here. Are you ready?"

"All set!"

"Let's go then. Good-bye, everybody."

"Good-bye!" every one shouted. Frank and Joe cheered, the girls clapped their hands, and the *Envoy* slowly moved away from the dock, with Chet Morton and Biff Hooper waving to their chums.

Tony Prito swung his motorboat around.

"I'll go along with you to the end of the bay," he shouted.

Frank glanced at Joe.

"Why didn't we think of that?"

"It isn't too late yet. Let's get the boat."

"Would you and Iola care to come?" said Frank to Callie. "We're going to get our boat and follow them down the bay a bit."

"Oh, that'll be great!" exclaimed Callie. "I'd love to go. Wouldn't you, Iola?"

"I'll say!" Iola replied, slangily.

They hurried down from the dock and went along the roadway back of the boathouses until they came to the boathouse where Frank and Joe kept their craft.

In a few minutes, the *Sleuth* was nosing its way out into Barmet Bay, but already Chet and Biff were a considerable distance in the lead.

"We'll have to step on it," said Joe.

"We'll catch them, all right. There isn't a boat on the bay can beat the *Sleuth*."

The engine roared and the boat seemed fairly to leap out of the water as it plunged forward. Spray dashed over the bows as the fleet launch headed out in pursuit of the others.

Frank glanced at the sky.

Biff and Chet had certainly chosen a bad day for their departure. The sky had been none too promising at dawn, but now it was clouding over with every promise of a downpour, and there was a heavy cloud on the horizon. Then, too, there was a suspicious absence of wind, and the bay was in a flat calm.

"I wish they'd picked some other day," he remarked quietly to Joe. "It looks like squally weather out at sea."

"I don't like the looks of the sky myself. However, they're away, so there's no use saying anything. It might alarm Iola."

The *Sleuth* was rapidly overhauling the other boats, although Tony and Biff were engaging in a spirited race down the bay. The girls enjoyed the swift progress and were laughing with excitement as they saw the distance narrowing between Frank and the others.

Suddenly a low rumble of thunder caused

Frank to glance up at the sky again. With remarkable rapidity, the huge cloud he had previously noticed had spread over the entire sky, causing gloom to spread over the bay. A few white caps were apparent on the surface of the water and there was a splatter of rain.

"Guess we'd better turn back," he said, turning to the others.

"Why, what's the matter?" asked Callie.

"Storm coming up."

The girls had been so intent on the chase that they had not noticed the lowering clouds, but now Callie gave a murmur of astonishment.

"Why, it's going to *pour!* And I haven't brought my slicker with me. We'll be drenched."

"But what about Biff and Chet?" exclaimed Iola.

"I think they'll turn back too when they see what they're heading into," replied Frank. "It looks like a bad storm."

As though in corroboration of his words, a sheet of lightning and a violent clap of thunder heralded the beginning of the downpour. The wind came in from the sea with a violence that surprised them, came whistling down across the bay over a wide line of tossing white-caps, driving before it a leaden wall of rain.

The two motorboats in the lead were blotted from view, although Frank had seen that Tony

Prito was already turning back before the gloomy wall of rain hid him from sight. Slowly, he brought the motorboat around.

The moaning of the wind rose in volume. Waves slapped at the sides of the boat. White spray rose above the bows. The sky was black. The speeding craft fled before the oncoming storm.

But the wall of rain swept down upon them with a whistle and a howl. The streaming sheets of water poured from the dark sky, whirled onward by the raging wind. The boat rocked in the tossing waves.

Frank crouched at the helm, his jaw set, his face stern. The girls huddled in the stern, seeking protection from the sudden downpour.

Joe found a sheet of tarpaulin in a locker, and gave it to the two girls, who draped it over their heads, and it afforded them some shelter. The boat was swaying madly as it ran on through the huge waves that surged on every side.

Frank could scarcely see Bayport ahead through the blinding rain and gloom.

"Where is the other boat?" shouted Joe, above the clamor of the storm.

Frank looked back.

Tony Prito's boat had disappeared. Frank wondered how the other boys were faring. He had every confidence that Tony would make land in safety, for the Italian lad was skilful at the helm and he had iron nerves, but he was not so sure that Biff Hooper and Chet Morton would weather the gale so easily. Biff had only mastered the rudiments of motorboating and a storm such as this was enough to test the mettle of the most skilful sailors.

He wondered if he should not turn back and go in search of Biff and Chet. When he had last seen them they had been heading directly into the teeth of the gale, out to the open sea. Surely they would not be foolhardy enough to go on!

He glanced back and when he saw Iola's frightened face he knew that it was impossible to turn back now, for he was responsible for the safety of the girls and there was grave peril in braving the storm just then. He opened the throttle further and felt the *Sleuth* respond as it leaped ahead into the tossing whitecaps through the shifting screen of rain.

Thunder rolled and crashed. Lightning flickered across the gray void and rent the dark sky in livid streaks. The waves were tossing like white-crested monsters seeking to devour them. Frank peered through the raging gale and he could vaguely discern the city lying ahead. A few lights were twinkling feebly, for the storm brought the darkness of twilight with it.

The gale had sprung up so suddenly that they had been entirely unprepared. Frank devoutly wished that he had taken heed of the warning given by that ominous sky before he started out in the motorboat. He was greatly alarmed for the safety of the girls, because he knew that the storm was one of the worst that had ever swept over Barmet Bay.

"We'll be lucky if we make it!" he muttered to himself. Then, to reassure the others, he turned and grinned.

"We'll make it, all right!" he shouted, the wind whisking the words away so that the others scarcely heard him.

A great wave broke over the side. The boat reeled as though it had been struck by a giant hand.

CHAPTER V

No Word from the Chums

FRANK HARDY bore down on the helm as the boat heeled over. For a breathless second he thought the craft would be swamped. Water poured over the gunwales. The girls screamed. Joe was thrown off his balance and went sprawling into the stern.

But the *Sleuth* was staunch. In a moment it recovered, righted itself, and surged on through the storm. Frank breathed a sigh of relief. The engine throbbed steadily and, although the boat was rocking and swaying in the turbulent sea, it was drawing nearer shore and already he could distinguish the line of boathouses through the downpour.

For all its violence, the storm was brief. The wind began to die down, although the rain continued as though the heavens had been opened up. In a few minutes Frank was able to pick out his own boathouse and he headed the *Sleuth* directly for it. The sturdy craft sped swiftly toward the open doorway, then

Frank shut off the engine and the boat came to rest.

"Some trip!" remarked Joe, shaking himself like a dog emerging from the water, so that spray flew from his clothing in every direction.

"My hair is all wet, and I won't be able to do a thing with it," mourned Callie Shaw, with feminine concern for her appearance first of all. In spite of the shelter afforded by the tarpaulin, both girls were thoroughly drenched. As for the boys, their clothing clung limply to their bodies. Frank clambered out of the boat and moored it fast, while Joe helped the girls up onto the landing.

"We're mighty lucky to be back at all," Iola Morton said. "I was sure the boat would be swamped."

"It takes a pretty big storm to swamp our boat," boasted Joe. "Although, to tell the truth, I was pretty nervous for a while."

"I was so frightened I couldn't speak," confessed the girl. "I do hope Chet and Biff turned back. They would never get through that storm alive."

Frank went to the door.

"No sight of them yet," he reported. Then he peered through the driving screen of rain again. "Just a minute—I hear a boat coming this way."

"Perhaps it's Tony."

"I hope it's one or the other. I couldn't see the *Napoli* at all after the rain started."

In a few minutes they discerned a motorboat heading inshore. It was Tony Prito's craft, the *Napoli*.

"Good!" exclaimed Joe. "Chet and Biff should be along, too. They won't start on that trip to-day."

"I should hope not!" exclaimed Iola.

But when Tony's boat drew near the entrance of the boathouse on the way to its own shelter a short distance away, Tony shouted to Frank:

"All safe?"

"Everybody O.K.! How about you?"

"We're all right. Had a tough time getting back, though."

"So did we," Frank shouted. "Did Biff turn back?"

Tony shook his head. "Not a chance. We signaled to him that he'd better come back but he just shook his head, and Chet pointed to the end of the bay. They kept right on going. The last we saw of them they were heading right into the storm."

"Good night!" Frank exclaimed. "They'll be swamped."

"They're taking an awful chance. Oh, well, perhaps they gave in after all. They may have headed in toward one of the villages along the shore. They'll probably be back."

"Let's hope so!" exclaimed Iola. "I won't have a minute's rest until I'm sure they're safe."

Tony went on toward his own boathouse, with Jerry Gilroy and Phil Cohen, drenched to the skin, sitting ruefully in the stern. The Hardy boys and the two girls left the boathouse and were fortunate enough to meet a school chum who happened to be driving past in his car, so they drove home in shelter from the rain. Frank and Joe got off at their home after the chum had volunteered to drive the girls home.

"And I'll make it snappy, too," he promised. "I guess you're in a hurry to get into dry clothes."

"I feel like a drowned rat," declared Callie. "And I suppose I look like one too."

After the others drove away, the Hardy boys went into the house and made a complete change of clothes so that, fifteen minutes later, in dry garments, they were feeling at peace with the world. When they went downstairs again to tell their parents of the adventure they had just experienced, they found Mr. Hardy just snapping the catch of his clubbag, while a packed suitcase stood near by.

"Going away now?" they asked, in surprise.

"Off to Chicago. I just got a fresh clue as to Baldy's whereabouts."

"He's there all right, is he?"

The detective nodded. "I'll just have time to catch this train."

Mrs. Hardy entered the room at that moment.

"I telephoned for a taxi." Her face was troubled. "I do wish you didn't have to make this journey, Fenton."

Mr. Hardy laughed.

"You've never worried about me so much before, Laura. I've gone away on cases as bad as this dozens of times without causing you as much anxiety."

"I know—but somehow I have a feeling that this case is a good deal more dangerous than any of the others."

"I'll be back in a few days, never fear." Mr. Hardy turned to his sons. "Look after your mother while I'm away, boys. Don't let her get worried."

"There's nothing to be worried about, dad. You'll get your man all right."

Mrs. Hardy shook her head. "You *will* be careful, won't you, Fenton? From what you've told me of this Baldy Turk I imagine he wouldn't stop at anything if he thought you were going to catch him."

"He's a pretty tough character, but I guess

I can handle him," said the detective lightly.
"Well, here's my taxi. I'll have to be going.
Good-bye." He kissed his wife, shook hands
with the boys, then picked up his suitcase and
club-bag and departed. From the front doorway they watched him clamber into the waiting
taxi. He waved at them as the car got under
way, then it went speeding out of sight along
the shimmering pavement.

Mrs. Hardy turned away. "I expect he'll
think I'm foolish for worrying so much about
him this time, but I have a queer sort of feeling that this Baldy Turk is the most dangerous
criminal he has ever had to deal with."

"He'll deal with him, mother," declared
Frank, with conviction. "Trust dad to know
what he's doing. He'll clap the handcuffs on
Baldy Turk in no time. There's nothing to
worry about."

"Well, I hope you're right," she replied.
"Still, I can't help but be anxious—"

With that she let the matter drop, and her
fears for Fenton Hardy's safety were not expressed again, although the boys knew that
anxiety still weighed heavily upon her mind.
By evening, however, she appeared to be in
better spirits and the boys did their best to
amuse her and make her forget their father's
absence and his perilous errand.

Next day the boys went down to the boat-

house where Biff Hooper kept the *Envoy,* but
there was no sign of the craft. The storm of
the previous day had lasted well into the
afternoon and there had been no doubt in their
minds but that Chet and Biff had set back for
Bayport, but the absence of the motorboat
indicated otherwise.

"Let's go up to Morton's farm and see if
they did come back," Frank suggested.

"Iola was saying that Chet promised to send
a post card from the first village they stopped
at. They were to have spent the night at Hawk
Cove and he said he'd drop a line from there
so that his folks would know everything was
all right."

Hawk Cove was a small fishing village on the
coast and, under normal conditions, Chet and
Biff should have reached the place early the
previous evening. A postal card would have
caught the morning mail to Bayport.

"Let's go, then," Frank said. "If they
went on to Hawk Cove and wrote from there
we'll know that everything is all right."

"I'm with you."

The Hardy boys brought their motorcycles
out of the shed and drove out toward the Morton farm. They made speed on the run because both were anxious to learn if anything
had been heard of their chums. But when
they reached the farmhouse and saw Iola's

worried face as she greeted them at the door they knew without being told that no word had been received from Chet.

"They didn't turn back," said Iola, almost tearfully. "We waited all afternoon and evening expecting Chet back, but he didn't come. They must have gone straight ahead into the storm."

"Did the post card come?" asked Joe.

She shook her head.

"We haven't heard from him at all. And Chet promised faithfully he'd write to us from Hawk Cove. The card should have been in the morning mail. Chet always keeps his promises. I'm so afraid something dreadful has happened."

"Oh, there's no need to be alarmed," consoled Frank. "Perhaps the storm delayed them so that they didn't reach Hawk Cove until it was too late to catch the mail. Or perhaps they stopped off at one of the other fishing villages down at the entrance to the bay. A dozen things might have happened. You'll probably hear from him to-morrow—or to-night, perhaps."

"That storm was too terrible!" declared the girl. "They should never have gone on. They should have turned back when the rest of us did."

"I guess they didn't want to turn back once

they had started," ventured Joe. "Biff doesn't like to admit he's licked."

"Neither does Chet," the girl replied. "They're both headstrong and I guess they thought we'd make fun of them if they had to come back to Bayport and start over again."

"Well, we'll be back to-morrow. I'm sure you'll hear from him by then," said Frank reassuringly. "And if we hear anything we'll let you know."

"Please do."

The Hardy boys walked back to their motor-cycles. When they were out of hearing Frank remarked in a low voice:

"I don't like the looks of this, at all! I'm beginning to think something *has* happened."

CHAPTER VI

MISSING

No WORD came from Chet Morton or Biff Hooper the following day. Although the parents of the chums tried to allay their fears by assuming that the lads had not stopped off at Hawk Cove after all or had neglected to write, as is the way of boys the world over, when three days passed without further news, the situation became serious.

"They were wrecked in that storm, I know it!" declared Iola Morton, with conviction, when the Hardy boys called at the farmhouse on the third day. "Mother is almost frantic and daddy doesn't know what to do. It isn't like Chet to make us wait this long for some word of where he is, particularly when he knew we'd be anxious."

"The Hoopers are terribly worried about Biff," Joe put in. "We went over there last night to see if they had heard anything. Mr. Hooper had telephoned to nearly all the fish-

ing villages up the coast, but none of them had
seen anything of the boat.''

Iola turned pale.

''They hadn't seen the boat at all?''

Frank shook his head.

''Either the boys were wrecked or they were
swept out to sea,'' said the girl. She turned
away and dabbled at her eyes with a handkerchief. She was on the verge of breaking
down. ''Oh, can't *something* be done to find
trace of them?''

''It's time we were getting busy,'' Frank
agreed. ''I think we'd better organize a
searching party.''

''With the motorboats?'' asked Joe.

''Yes. We can take our boat. Perhaps
Tony Prito will be able to come along with the
Napoli and we'll get the rest of the fellows.
We can cruise along the bay and up the coast
and perhaps we'll find some trace.''

''Will you do that?'' asked Iola, brightening
up. ''Oh, if you only will! At least we'll know
that some one is searching for them.''

''I've been thinking that possibly their boat
got wrecked and they were washed up on an
island or on some part of the coast a long way
from any village,'' Frank observed. ''I don't
think they've been drowned. They are both
good swimmers and it would take a lot to kill
either of them.''

"Well, if we're going to go we may as well get started."

"All right, Joe. We'll take some grub with us and count on staying until we find some trace of them. Perhaps two or three days."

A sudden thought struck Joe.

"How about mother?"

Frank whistled.

"Gosh—I'd forgotten! But perhaps she can get some one to stay with her. Seeing it isn't a pleasure trip we're going on, she might let us go."

"Oh, I hope she does!" exclaimed Iola. "As long as we know you boys are out searching for Chet and Biff we'll be a lot easier in our minds."

"Well, let's go back home and see what arrangements we can make," Frank said briskly. "The sooner we get away, the better."

The lads mounted their motorcycles and turned toward the city. The idea of organizing a searching party for the missing chums had occurred to Frank previously, but he had been waiting, hoping against hope that some word might be received regarding the two boys. The fact that Mrs. Hardy would be left alone at home had been the one circumstance that had prevented him from starting out in search of the chums before this, but now the situation seemed to warrant action at all costs.

"If mother is afraid to stay at home alone, I guess the trip is off," he said to Joe. "But when she knows how serious it is, I don't think she'll mind."

"I don't like to leave her alone, myself," replied Joe. "But some one has to organize a searching party. I've been more worried about Chet and Biff than I'd like to admit."

"Me too."

When the lads returned to the house they found Mrs. Hardy opening the morning mail. She had a letter in her hand as they entered the living room and she glanced up with a smile of pleasure.

"We're going to have a visitor."

"Who?"

"Your Aunt Gertrude!"

Frank glanced at his brother.

Well did they know their Aunt Gertrude. She was a maiden lady of middle-age who spent the greater part of her life in a sort of grand circuit series of visits to all her relatives, far and near. Aunt Gertrude had no fixed place of abode. Accompanied by numerous trunks, satchels and a lazy yellow cat by the name of Lavinia, she was apt to drop in at any time in the course of a year, brusquely announcing her intention of remaining for an indefinite stay. Then she would install herself in the guest room and proceed to manage the household until the hour of her departure.

Aunt Gertrude was formidable. Her word was law. And, because she was possessed of a small fortune and a sharp tongue, none dared offend her. Relatives had discovered that the best plan was to suffer her visits in silence and pray for her speedy departure.

Now she was coming to visit the Hardys.

"Aunt Gertrude is coming? Isn't that great?" exclaimed Joe.

Mrs. Hardy looked at her son suspiciously. The Hardy boys had never been known to evince much enthusiasm over Aunt Gertrude's visits before. The worthy lady had a habit of regarding them as though they were still in swaddling clothes and she invariably showed a tendency to dictate as to their food, their hours of rising and going to bed, their companions, and their choice of literature. Many a Sunday afternoon she had thrust on them a weighty volume of Pilgrim's Progress and sat guard over them as they miserably strove to pretend an interest in the allegorical adventures of Bunyan's hero.

"I didn't think you cared for Aunt Gertrude," ventured Mrs. Hardy when she saw that both Frank and Joe were beaming with satisfaction.

"When will she be here?"

"This afternoon, according to her letter.

She never gives one a great deal of notice.''

''She couldn't have come at a better time. For once in her life, Aunt Gertrude will be useful,'' Frank declared, and with that, he told his mother of their desire to organize a searching party for the missing chums.

Mrs. Hardy had been deeply concerned over Chet and Biff since their departure from Bayport and now she agreed that a search should indeed be conducted.

''And now that Aunt Gertrude is coming, you won't be afraid to stay here alone,'' Joe pointed out.

Mrs. Hardy smiled. ''And you'll leave me here all alone to the mercies of that managing woman?''

''There's not much use having us *all* here. Aunt Gertrude will run things anyway, whether there's three of us or a hundred.''

''Yes, I suppose so. Well, I shan't be afraid to stay here as long as Aunt Gertrude is in the house. I imagine any burglar would rather deal with a vicious bulldog. Go ahead on your trip. When do you intend to start?''

''As soon as we can see Tony Prito and the rest of the boys. We want to make a real searching party of it. By the way, when will Aunt Gertrude arrive?''

''On the four o'clock train, I expect.''

''Then we'll leave at about three o'clock,''

declared Frank, with a grin, for the boys' dislike of their tyrannical aunt was no secret in the Hardy household.

Mrs. Hardy smiled reprovingly, and the lads hustled away in search of Tony and the other boys.

Tony Prito was afire with enthusiasm when they broached the subject to him. A few words with Mr. Prito, and he obtained permission to have the use of the *Napoli* for as long as would be necessary.

"We'll start out as soon as we can get ready," Frank told him. "See if you can get Jerry and Phil to go with you, and we'll go and look up Perry Robinson. Perhaps he'll come along with us. We don't want to lose any time."

Perry Robinson, more familiarly known as "Slim," readily agreed to accompany the boys on the search.

"You bet I'll go," he declared. "When do we start?"

"Three o'clock, if we can be ready by then. Meet us at the boathouse and bring along some grub."

"I'll be there," promised Slim.

The Hardy boys carried blankets and a small tent down to the boat and stowed them away. Then came cooking utensils and a supply of food sufficient to last them for several days.

They would, of course, be able to get supplies at the fishing villages along the coast, but as they had no idea where their search would lead them they were determined to take no chances.

"Thank goodness we'll be away from here before Aunt Gertrude arrives," chuckled Frank, as the boys were putting on their outing clothes at two o'clock that afternoon.

"She'll be madder than a wet hen when she finds we've escaped her. If there's anything she likes better than bossing us around and showing us our faults, I don't know what it is."

Alas for the best laid plans! Aunt Gertrude must have had some premonition of the truth. She advanced the time of her arrival by a good two hours. The two o'clock train brought her to Bayport, bags, baggage, and Lavinia, the cat. The boys were first apprised of her advent when they heard a taxicab pull up in front of the house. Joe peeped out the window of their room.

"Sweet spirits of nitre! Aunt Gertrude herself!"

"No!"

"Yes!"

"Let me see!"

Frank rushed to the window in time to see Aunt Gertrude, attired in voluminous garments of a fashion dating back at least a

decade, laboriously emerging from the taxicab. She was a large woman with a strident
voice, and the Hardy boys could hear her vigorously disputing the amount of the fare. This
was a matter of principle with Aunt Gertrude,
who always argued with taxi drivers as a
matter of course, it being her firm conviction
that they were unanimously in a conspiracy to
overcharge her and defraud her at all times.

With Lavinia under one arm and a huge
umbrella under the other, Aunt Gertrude
withered the taxicab driver with a fiery denun-
ciation and, when he helplessly pointed to the
meter and declared that figures did not lie, she
dropped both cat and umbrella, rummaged
about in the manifold recesses of her clothing
for a very small purse, produced the exact
amount of the fare in silver, counted it out
and handed it to the man with the air of one
giving alms.

"And, just for your impudence, you shan't
have a tip!" she announced. "Carry my bags
up to the house."

The driver gazed sadly at the silver in his
hand, pocketed it and clambered back into the
car.

"Carry 'em up yourself!" he advised,
slamming the door. The taxi roared away
down the street.

Frank chuckled.

"That's one on Aunt Gertrude!"

But Aunt Gertrude had no intention of carrying the bags up to the house. Suddenly she glared up at the window from which the two boys had been watching the scene.

"You two boys up there!" she shouted. "I see you. Don't think I can't see you! Come down here and carry up my bags. Hustle now!"

They hustled.

CHAPTER VII

WRECKAGE

"GOOD night! We'll be lucky if we get away on the trip at all!" exclaimed Frank, as he and Joe hastened down the stairs.

Mrs. Hardy was already at the front door welcoming Aunt Gertrude, who was expatiating on the wickedness of taxi drivers in general.

"So!" she ejaculated, as the boys appeared. "Standing up at a front window laughing at your great-aunt instead of coming down and helping carry up her bags like little gentlemen! I'm surprised at you!"

"We were just getting dressed, Aunt Gertrude," explained Frank meekly.

"Getting dressed, eh!" snorted Aunt Gertrude, taking in their attire. "Getting dressed! What kind of an outfit do you call that?" She poked Joe in the ribs with her umbrella, indicating the faded khaki shirt he was wearing "Speak up, boy! What kind of an outfit is that? No necktie. Holes in your trousers. Shoes not shined."

"We were just getting ready to go on a boat trip, Aunt Gertrude," Joe explained.

"Boat trip! Boat trip! No! That settles it!" declared Aunt Gertrude, coming into the house and banging the umbrella decisively on the floor by way of emphasis. "I shan't allow it. The very idea! Laura," she said, turning to Mrs. Hardy, "I'm surprised at you. Abso-lute-ly astonished! The very idea of letting these children go out in a boat! Don't you remember what happened to my Cousin Peter? He went out in a boat, didn't he? And what happened? The boat upset. He might have been drowned if the water had been deep enough. Thank goodness he was only a few feet from shore. But it only goes to show what *can* happen. If these boys go out in a boat they'll be drowned. I can't permit them to be drowned. They shan't go on any boat trip. That settles it!" She strode into the living room. "Boys—bring in my bags!" she commanded.

Mrs. Hardy smiled, for she was quite accustomed to the eccentricities of Aunt Gertrude, and the Hardy boys scuttled down the front steps for the baggage.

"Do you think she means it?" whispered Joe.

"Sure, she means it. But we'll get out somehow. She'll rave for a while, but she'll forget all about it when she starts to show mother how to run the house."

The boys deposited Aunt Gertrude's luggage in the guest room, then went downstairs for inspection. By this time the old lady had taken off her coat and hat and was seated in the most comfortable chair, fanning herself with a newspaper.

"Boat trip!" she was snorting, as they entered the room. "Never heard of such a thing. Letting little boys like that go out in a boat alone. If they were *my* boys I wouldn't let them out of my sight. Up to some mischief, I'll be bound."

"They are going out to look for two chums of theirs who have been lost for three days," Mrs. Hardy explained.

"And serve them right! I suppose they were out on a boat trip, too. I knew it! And now they're lost. That's what happens when you let children go out in boats. They get lost. Or drowned. And now you would let these two youngsters go out in a boat, too. And I suppose in a few days some of their chums would have to go out in a boat to look for *them*. They'd get lost, too. And then some more little boys would go out to look for *them*. And they'd get lost. By the end of the summer there wouldn't be a boy left in Bayport. Not that it would be much of a loss," sniffed Aunt Gertrude; "but I hate to see people making fools of themselves."

"Did you have a pleasant journey?" asked Mrs. Hardy, anxious to change the subject.

"Did I *ever* have a pleasant journey?" countered Aunt Gertrude. "What with the rudeness of conductors and ticket-sellers and baggage-men and taxi drivers there's no enjoyment in traveling nowadays. But *I* put 'em in their place. I know my rights and I insist on them!"

She glared ferociously about the room as though confronting a multitude of conductors, baggage-men and taxi drivers awaiting judgment.

"Now, boys! what are you staring at? Don't you know it's rude to be staring at people? Run away and play. I want to talk to your mother. Run away and play! Shoo!" She brandished the umbrella at them and the Hardy boys left the room precipitately. Their mother excused herself for a moment and followed them into the hall.

"Run!" she said, smiling. "I'll take care of Aunt Gertrude. Run along while you have the chance."

They kissed their mother good-bye and hastily departed, wondering how she was to explain their flight to the terrible Aunt Gertrude, in view of that lady's melancholy predictions concerning their fate should they venture out in the boat.

They found Slim Robinson waiting for them at the boathouse, and with many chuckles the boys told him of their escape from the tyrant who would have prevented their departure.

"We'd better hurry or she'll be down here after us if she finds we've got away from her," declared Joe.

"Tony and the other fellows are over in the other boathouse," Slim told them. "I think they're ready now."

"All right. Let's be going."

Frank started the engine of the *Sleuth* and the motorboat moved slowly out into the open bay. He steered a course for the entrance to Prito's boathouse, where Tony and the others were waiting. As soon as Tony saw him he started his own craft, and the *Napoli* nosed its way out abreast of them.

"All set?" shouted Frank.

"All set."

"Away we go."

The two boats drummed their way out into Barmet Bay and headed out toward the sea, side by side, picking up speed when they had threaded their way through the shipping near the docks.

It was evening before they reached the first village on the coast, after leaving the bay, and although they made numerous inquiries they failed to find any trace of their chums. No one in the village had seen or heard a motorboat during the storm, although they readily admitted that the craft might have passed without being noticed, owing to the gloom and the violence of the gale. The chums spent the night at this village and resumed their journey the next morning, going farther up the coast.

Their progress was necessarily slow because there were numerous small villages and they stopped at them all to make inquiries.

But in every case the answer was the same.

No motorboat answering to the description of the *Envoy* had been seen. None of the fishermen had heard of the craft.

"It's ten chances to one that they was wrecked in that storm," an old fisherman at one of the villages declared when they told him their story. "Unless they were mighty lucky they wouldn't get past Ragged Reef. They might get this far up the coast, but they'd never get past the Reef."

"Where is that?"

"Not far from here. Up past the next point. Seems to me I heard one of the boys sayin' this mornin' that there was some wreckage on the reef yesterday. There's none of our boats missin' from hereabouts, so mebby it's them young fellers.''

The two motorboats thereupon started for Ragged Reef. The lads were downhearted. They had little hope that they would ever find their two companions alive. The words of the old fisherman struck terror into their hearts.

When they rounded the point they saw the black and ominous line of Ragged Reef before them. A jagged and irregular series of rocks jutting above the surface of the water in the form of a huge semicircle—this was the reef on which the *Envoy* might have come to grief.

Fortunately, the day was calm so that the searchers were able to venture more closely to the reef than they might have otherwise dared. Frank edged the *Sleuth* in toward the rocks as closely as possible. Suddenly he gave an exclamation:

''The fisherman was right! There *is* wreckage there!''

He pointed to a few broken fragments of wood that could be discerned against the rocks. Joe picked up the marine glasses and peered at the fragments for some time.

''It's wreckage of a boat of some kind,'' he declared gravely, lowering the glasses at last. ''But whether it's from the *Envoy* or not, I couldn't say.''

Slim also looked through the glasses. He

was able to see more fragments of wreckage farther along the reef.

"Some boat has been battered to pieces along here.   There isn't enough wreckage left to tell whether it was a motorboat or a sailing vessel." He scrutinized the mainland. "Nothing there," he announced finally. "Not a sign of life—nor wreckage either. It's all on the reef."

So interested had the boys been in the fragments of broken wood on the jagged rocks that they had not noticed that the motorboat was edging in closer to the reef.   There was a strong current at this point and, unnoticed by the boys, the boat was being carried irresistibly forward.

A warning shout from the lads in the *Napoli* told them of their danger.

Frank had throttled down the engine so that the *Sleuth* had been almost drifting. Now he sprang for the helm, conscious of the peril that had crept so insidiously upon them.

The great black rocks of the reef loomed closer. The motorboat seemed to be dragged mercilessly toward its doom. The powerful current had the craft firmly in its grasp!

CHAPTER VIII

The Strange Letter

The engine roared as Frank Hardy opened the throttle and bore down on the helm of the *Sleuth*.

The grip of the current about the reef was so strong that, for a moment, it seemed that the motorboat could not fight against it. Then, slowly, the craft swung about, seemed to remain motionless for a moment, and then began to forge ahead, away from the reef.

Fighting against the force of the current, the motorboat made slow progress. Still, it was gaining ground. The boys waited tensely, as the craft struggled out of danger. Gradually, the *Sleuth* drew away from the reef, gradually the grip of the current relaxed. Frank cautiously nosed the boat over to the left and managed to get out of the current altogether.

The whole affair had occurred in a few seconds, but it had seemed an eternity to the boys in the boat and their chums in the other craft. It would only have been a matter of moments before they might have been swept swiftly down onto the treacherous reef.

"That'll teach me to watch where I'm going," said Frank, as he sat back and mopped his brow.

"There was mighty near a lot more wreckage on that reef," remarked Slim soberly. "The boat wouldn't have lasted long if we'd piled up on those rocks."

"I'll say it wouldn't! I think we'd better get away from here. We'll never be able to get close enough to identify that wreckage. Might as well go on up the coast."

They drew up alongside the *Napoli* and, after discussing the narrow escape they had just had from being cast up on the reef, acquainted the other boys with their decision to continue the search.

"There's no use trying to get closer to that wreckage," declared Frank. "It's all in small pieces and we probably wouldn't be able to say whether it was from the *Envoy* or not, if we did reach it. We may as well go on up the coast and keep making inquiries at the other villages."

This plan they followed, but to no avail.

Their inquiries were fruitless. The *Envoy,* with Chet and Biff, seemed to have vanished into thin air. At none of the fishing villages were they able to find any one who had seen

or heard of the missing motorboat. As for
the wreckage on the reef, no one was found who
could enlighten them. Two or three fishing
boats had been wrecked during the storm, but
they had met their fate farther up the coast
and in each case the scene of the wreck was
known to the fishermen.

"It might have been your friend's boat, and
it might have been only some old wreckage
washed down the coast by the storm," said
one keen-eyed salt. "You'd best give up the
search. If they're drowned, they're drowned,
and that's all there is to it. If they were
wrecked and managed to save themselves
they'll make their way to the nearest village
and they'll get home from there without any
trouble. If you haven't found any trace of
them by now there isn't much use going any
further, for they would never have got this far
up the coast having been seen by some of the
fishermen."

The boys reluctantly agreed that his advice
was sound. They turned back for Bayport.

When they returned to the city and reported
that their quest had been unsuccessful they
were scarcely prepared for the sensation that
the news aroused. The Hoopers were frantic
with anxiety, as their last hopes were dashed.
The Mortons were almost stunned. They had
hoped against hope that the search would

bring them at least some news of the missing boys.

The local papers featured the story and the city was aroused. In every village and town along the coast, to north and south, people were discussing the mysterious disappearance of the motorboat and its human freight. Fishermen were on the lookout for any trace of the craft. The coast guards promised to do all in their power to clear up the mystery.

But, when three days more went by and there was still not the slightest solution in sight, the opinion became general that the boat had been wrecked in the storm and had gone to the bottom. The two boys were given up for lost. The Hardy boys and their chums were gradually forced to the belief that Chet and Biff had perished.

Then came an incident that temporarily drove the tragic affair from the minds of Frank and Joe, because it concerned their own home more intimately.

Aunt Gertrude had greeted them on their return with a barrage of scathing comment on their disobedience in leaving on the trip in spite of her avowed disapproval, and she expressed the greatest amazement because they had returned alive after all.

"You may thank Providence that you got back," she declared in her characteristically brusque fashion. "It was through no skill of your own, I'll be bound. Your poor mother and me were worried to death all the time you were away—gallivanting over the ocean."

Aunt Gertrude did not add that Mrs. Hardy's worries had been chiefly occasioned by her aunt's dire predictions of the certain death that awaited the boys on the search. However, her tone was modified somewhat when she realized that they had indeed been hunting for the missing chums and she made it her business to call on the Hoopers and the Mortons to condole with them, for she was a good-hearted soul in her own way—although it is to be feared that her condolences did more to add to the certainty that the boys were drowned than they served to cheer up the sorrowing parents.

The third day after the Hardy boys returned she was sorting over the morning mail, having duly taken charge of every department of the household.

"Ha!" she exclaimed, holding a letter up to the light. "Here's a letter addressed to Fenton Hardy. Bad news in it, I'll be bound."

Aunt Gertrude could smell bad news a mile away, Frank often said.

"Bad news in it. I can tell. I dreamed about haystacks last night. Haystacks! Whenever I dream about haystacks it means bad news. I never knew it to fail. Open the letter, Laura."

"But it isn't addressed to me," objected Mrs. Hardy.

"Fiddlesticks! It's addressed to your husband, isn't it? You have as much right to open it as he has. More. It's a wife's duty to help her husband as much as she can and look after his affairs for him. Man and wife are one, aren't they? Open the letter."

Mrs. Hardy, with some misgivings, slit open the envelope and Aunt Gertrude, who was possessed of an insatiable curiosity, immediately seized the letter.

"I'll read it for you!" she offered.

"'Fenton Hardy—Bayport,'" she began. "'Dear Sir: We wish to inform you that we have—' My goodness! What's this? What's this? Gracious me!" She lapsed into unintelligible mutterings as she read the rest of the letter to herself, frequently giving vent to exclamations of surprise while her eyes widened with astonishment.

Mrs. Hardy and the boys could hardly contain their impatience until at last Aunt Gertrude laid down the letter and peered triumphantly at them over her spectacles.

"Didn't I say so?" she demanded stridently. "Didn't I say there was bad news in this letter? Didn't I tell you I dreamed of haystacks last night? Haystacks always mean bad news." She looked at the letter again. "Although for the life of me I can't imagine what the man means. Hum! Kidnapped!" She looked up suddenly at the Hardy boys and glared at them.

"You boys haven't been kidnapped lately? No. Of course not. What nonsense! Has any one tried to kidnap you?"

"No, Aunt Gertrude," said Frank, utterly mystified.

"Then," demanded Aunt Gertrude, pushing the letter across to Mrs. Hardy and folding her arms as though prepared to wait until doomsday for a satisfactory answer, "what does this letter mean?"

Mrs. Hardy picked up the letter and read it aloud, while an expression of amazement crossed her face.

"Fenton Hardy—Bayport," ran the letter. "Dear Sir: We wish to inform you that we are holding your two sons in a safe place and that we will not return them to you unless you agree to the following conditions: You must pay us the sum of $5000 as ransom, you must agree to refuse to give evidence in the Asbury Park bank robbery case, and you must further agree to give up your pursuit of our leader, Baldy Turk. These are our conditions. It will do you no good to attempt to find your sons, for we will not hesitate to put them out of the way if you attempt to discover our hiding place. Furthermore, unless you agree to what we ask, it will go hard with them. You may signify your agreement to the terms of this letter by dropping a package containing the money and a signed statement to the effect that you will drop your pursuit of Baldy Turk and that you will not give evidence against our associates in the robbery case from the 5:15 express from Bayport next Thursday afternoon as it passes the grade crossing at the North Road.''

The letter was unsigned.

"What on earth does it mean?" asked Mrs. Hardy.

Frank and Joe looked at one another in astonishment. Frank reached over for the letter and examined it. The strange document was typewritten on an ordinary quality of white paper. The envelope bore the Bayport postmark, indicating that it had been mailed from the city post-office early that morning.

"It must be a practical joke of some kind," said Mrs. Hardy, in perplexity.

"Practical joke, nothing!" scoffed Aunt Gertrude shrewdly. "Did Fenton Hardy go to Chicago after some criminal?"

"He went to arrest Baldy Turk," replied Frank.

"There!" Aunt Gertrude pounded the table.

"That explains the whole thing. The companions of this Baldy person sent that letter in the hope that it would bring Fenton Hardy back from Chicago by the next train."

"But the letter is addressed to Bayport."

"Certainly! Why not? They wouldn't know where to reach him in Chicago, so they sent the letter here and trusted that it would be forwarded to him. And if *I* hadn't been here," said Aunt Gertrude, "it very probably *would* have been forwarded to him. Am I right?"

"I usually forward his personal mail," admitted Mrs. Hardy.

"There! Didn't I know it? And look what would have happened. Fenton Hardy would have fallen right into the trap. He would have come back home, thinking his precious sons were kidnapped, and that would have given this Turk person time to get away. It's a blessing I was here, I tell you. I hope this will be a lesson to you, Laura Hardy. *Always open your husband's mail!* Always!"

CHAPTER IX

BLACKSNAKE ISLAND

IN spite of Aunt Gertrude's ingenious explanation of the letter, the Hardy boys were not quite satisfied. When they left the house they walked downtown, discussing the matter.

"Aunt Gertrude may be right, but somehow I think those fellows sent the letter to the house, believing dad was still there," declared Joe.

"But if they knew he was at the house, or thought he was at the house, he would know we weren't kidnapped."

"Yes, that's right," Joe admitted, puzzled. "I'm hanged if I can figure it out, but I still think there is more to that letter than Aunt Gertrude imagines."

"I have that idea myself. You noticed that they were very particular to tell how the ransom money was to be delivered. That was quite an elaborate stunt, to have the money thrown off the train at a grade crossing. That would mean that the crooks could come along in a car, snatch up the package and be away without

74

much risk of capture. They'd hardly go to the
trouble of outlining all that if they didn't mean
something by it.''

"Yes, if the letter was only sent as a blind to
bring dad back to Bayport you'd hardly think
they'd go into all that detail.''

"Still,'' Frank pointed out, "here we are,
safe and sound. Haven't been kidnapped yet,
and nobody has tried to kidnap us. If that letter had been sent to Chet's people, for instance,
or to the Hoopers, they would have something
to worry about.'' Suddenly he stopped and
looked at Joe. "Say!'' he exclaimed.
"There's an idea!''

"What?''

"Chet and Biff!'' declared Frank excitedly.
"Don't you see? This may have something to
do with them. Chet and Biff are missing. Perhaps *they* have been kidnapped.''

"But why should any one kidnap them?''
Joe looked wonderingly at his brother.

"In mistake for us. Don't you see it? Perhaps this gang mistook Chet and Biff for you
and me and kidnapped them! Then they wrote
the letter to dad.''

"Gee, I never thought of that!'' Joe exclaimed. "I'll bet dollars to doughnuts that
you're right.''

"Don't you remember the day we were all
out in the boat and the three men came so close

to us? Remember how closely they looked at Chet and Biff? Perhaps those fellows had been tipped off that you and I were in the boat and wanted to get a look at us so they could identify us when they got a chance to kidnap us. And instead of looking at us, they picked on Chet and Biff. They knew we owned a boat, but they wouldn't know that Biff had one. Therefore they'd think that the chap at the wheel would be either you or me."

"It hangs together, all right. And then, remember when we saw those same three men hanging around the Morton farm? They must have trailed Chet home to see where he lived. And all the time they thought he was either you or me!"

"I think we're getting at the truth of it, Joe. When Chet and Biff started on their trip, those fellows followed them or lay in wait for them some place and captured them."

Just then the Hardy boys met Phil Cohen and Tony Prito in front of the fruit stand of their friend, Nick the Greek, each with a bottle of pop.

"Hello," was Tony's greeting. "Have one?" he invited, indicating the pop.

"Don't mind if we do, even if it is just after breakfast."

Nick the Greek dexterously opened two bottles of pop and slapped them down on the counter. "Hot day, eh?" he said, as the boys reached for straws.

"You bet it's hot." After a satisfying gurgle of the ice-cold pop, the Hardy boys turned to their chums. "We have a clue," declared Frank.

"About what?"

"About Chet and Biff."

"Yes?" Tony and Phil were immediately interested. "What's up?"

Frank then told them of the incident of the letter and, often prompted by his brother, explained how they had connected it with the disappearance of their chums.

"And so," he concluded, "we've figured that Chet and Biff may have been kidnapped in mistake for us."

"There's something in that, too," agreed Phil. "And here's something else that may help. I forgot about it when we were searching for the fellows the other day. Just a little while before they went on their trip I was talking to Chet and Biff and I remember that Biff said he had always wanted to visit Blacksnake Island."

"Blacksnake Island!" exclaimed Frank. "That's the place that is overrun with big blacksnakes, isn't it? Nobody ever goes there."

"That's the place, and that's why it's called

Blacksnake Island. And you can't blame people for staying away from it—with a name like that. But Biff had read about it and said he wanted to see what the place was like.''

"That's Biff all over," agreed Tony. "But did they decide to go?"

"Chet didn't want to go. Blacksnake Island is down the coast, and Chet wanted to go up the coast.''

"Sure! That's why we searched up the coast—because Chet said that was where they were going!" Frank declared.

"Well, Biff kept on saying that he wanted to see Blacksnake Island anyway, and while Chet wasn't very much struck with the idea he *might* have gone there.''

"Perhaps they went that way after all. I wish we'd known that when we made our first search. They might have started for Blacksnake Island and got captured on the way." Frank drained the last of his bottle of pop. "Say, I'd like to start another search for them, and go down the coast in that direction. What do you say?"

"I guess I can get away all right," said Tony. "How about you, Phil?"

"It's O.K. with me.''

"We'll probably find it hard to get away," said Frank doubtfully. "We'll go home and ask mother, anyway. You see, we're supposed to stay around the house now that dad's away. But Aunt Gertrude is there and if we can make a getaway without her seeing us I guess it'll be all right.''

"Look us up if you can make it.''

"You bet we will! Let's go home now, Joe, and see if we can go.''

The boys separated and Frank and Joe returned home. They found their mother and Aunt Gertrude still discussing the letter.

"It's absolute foolishness, Laura Hardy, that's all it is!'' Aunt Gertrude declared. "You'll just scare the man out of his wits and he'll be back here on the first train.''

"Well, I've sent the message, and at least I'll know where he is. I haven't had any word from Fenton since he left and it's been making me nervous.''

"Fiddlesticks! The man is too busy to write.''

"It isn't like him not to drop a line every two or three days. He is usually very particular about it. He always sends me a note at least twice a week while he's away.''

"Well,'' sighed Aunt Gertrude, as though giving it up as a bad job, "I suppose you know your own affairs best; but I'm telling you I would *not* have sent that telegram. There!'' and she picked up her knitting, the needles flashing furiously.

"What's the matter?" asked Frank.

"Little boys should be seen and not heard," grunted Aunt Gertrude, glaring at him over the tops of her spectacles.

"I sent a telegram to your father, telling him about the letter," their mother explained. "I think he should know about it. And, besides, I've been worrying because he hasn't written."

"Where did you address the telegram?"

"He gave me two addresses where I would be sure to find him in Chicago," said Mrs. Hardy. "He gave me the name of the hotel he would be staying at and he also said that Police Headquarters would reach him. I sent the same telegram to each place so I'd be sure to get him."

"Waste of money," sniffed Aunt Gertrude.

At that moment the telephone rang. Mrs. Hardy answered it. The 'phone was in the hallway and the boys could not hear their mother's words, but when she returned to the room a few minutes later they saw that she was pale with apprehension.

"The telegraph company tells me that there is no Fenton Hardy registered at the hotel and that Police Headquarters say he hasn't shown up there either," she announced gravely.

The boys looked at each other in surprise.

"That's strange," said Frank. "And he

hasn't written.   There's something mighty
queer about this!''

Aunt Gertrude, for once, was at a loss for
words.   The knitting needles remained sus-
pended in mid-air.   Behind the spectacles, her
eyes were wide and her mouth remained open in
astonishment.

"This affair gets more puzzling every minute,'' remarked Frank, at last.   "Of course dad
might have been delayed, or he might have
picked up a clue that took him away from Chicago after all.   But I think he would have written.''

"Perhaps he didn't report at Police Headquarters in Chicago because he was afraid
Baldy Turk's gang might find out he was in the
city,'' Joe suggested.

"There's something in that.''

"But why wouldn't he be at the hotel?'' asked
Mrs. Hardy.

"He might be there under an assumed name.
If Baldy Turk's gang are on the lookout for
him he wouldn't register under his real name.
They would be checking up on all the hotels to
find him if they thought he was in Chicago,''
said Frank eagerly.   "Perhaps that's why your
message didn't reach him.''

"Of course, that's why!'' sniffed Aunt Gertrude, returning to her knitting, much relieved.
"Any one might have known that.   It was a

waste of time to try to reach him with a telegram, and I said that from the start.'' The needles clashed.

''Oh, I guess we needn't worry about dad very much. He can look after himself,'' said Frank, with a warning glance at his brother. Nevertheless, he was deeply worried over the fact that the telegraph company had failed to locate his father. However, he was trying to make light of the matter so as to relieve his mother of worry.

Joe saw his motive.

''Sure, dad can look after himself. There's nothing to be alarmed about. He's probably keeping out of sight in Chicago for fear Baldy Turk's gang will find out he is there. If they ever knew he was on their trail they wouldn't stop at trying to kill him. He said so himself. If he tried to communicate with us it might give them just the clue they are waiting for.''

''I suppose you're right,'' Mrs. Hardy agreed, brightening up. ''Well, we won't worry about it.''

''Of course we won't worry about it!'' declared Aunt Gertrude. ''Worry is unhealthy. Worry has sent more people to their graves than anything else. Look at me. I never worry. That's why I'm so healthy. I'll live to be a hundred.''

''Yes, it would take quite a lot to kill you,

Aunt Gertrude,'' agreed Frank innocently.

Aunt Gertrude looked up at him suspiciously.

"I don't know just what you mean by that, young man, but I'll warrant there's something behind it! What are you two rascals waiting around here for, anyway? What do you want?"

"We were just wanting to talk to mother."

"Well, go ahead. Who's stopping you? *I* won't listen, I'm sure. If it's none of my business you needn't be afraid that *I'll* listen. Not at all. Not at all. Go right ahead. Talk to your mother if you wish. Of course, if you want to leave your poor old aunt out of everything I'm sure *I* don't mind. I'm not interested, anyway."

Whereupon Aunt Gertrude indignantly hitched her chair around toward the window and knitted vigorously.

"Go ahead! I'm not listening. Talk away. I won't listen to a word of it," she shrilled.

Mrs. Hardy smiled.

"What is it, boys?"

"I'm not listening," declared Aunt Gertrude.

"We think we've found a new clue about Chet and Biff," said Frank. "We wanted to go on another search for them!"

"What!" shrieked Aunt Gertrude, quite

forgetting that she had not been listening She wheeled about in her chair. "Go on another search for those two boys! Of all the idiotic ideas! Laura Hardy, if you let these two children go gallivanting out into the ocean again it will be against my advice."

"Where are you planning to look for them?" asked Mrs. Hardy.

"Blacksnake Island!"

Aunt Gertrude gasped. In her astonishment she dropped her knitting needles. "Blacksnake Island! Frank Hardy, have you gone completely off your head?"

CHAPTER X

The Boy on the Deck

Perhaps it was because Mrs. Hardy was determined to show that she was mistress in her own home. At any rate, she gave her consent to the proposed expedition. This was in spite of all Aunt Gertrude's protests and predictions of disaster. The terrible woman raved for an hour when it was definitely decided that the Hardy boys should go on the trip, but Mrs. Hardy was firm. If there was any chance that they might be able to rescue Chet and Biff she meant that they should avail themselves of it.

They explained their theory regarding the letter, and although Aunt Gertrude derided it as nonsense, Mrs. Hardy was disposed to believe that their deductions might be correct.

"You may go," she said. "But take care of yourselves and don't take any foolish chances. I'm worrying enough about your father, as it is."

So the boys left the house before Aunt Gertrude would have an opportunity to change their mother's mind and joyfully acquainted Phil and Tony with the news.

"We're going to start right away," they told their chums. "Better get ready."

"I was speaking to Slim Robinson and Jerry Gilroy," Tony told them. "They want to come along too."

"There isn't room for all of us in the one boat."

"I was thinking of that. What's the matter with the rest of us making the trip in the *Napoli?* I'll get up another expedition and we'll follow you."

"Good idea. One of the boys can come with us and the rest of you can go in the *Napoli.* Joe and I are starting right away."

But when it came time to check up on the various members of the searching party they discovered that Tony was the only one who could leave that day. Slim Robinson had to work that afternoon, as also had Jerry Gilroy, while Phil Cohen had an engagement for the evening that he was unable to break.

"We'll all leave in the *Napoli* first thing to-morrow morning, then," decided Tony. "You and Joe go ahead in your boat now and head toward Blacksnake Island. We'll be along in the morning."

This was the plan agreed upon, and the Hardy boys lost no time in making ready for the trip. They had the forethought to stock up with provisions for several days, although the run to Blacksnake Island would not take them many hours, because they realized that the search might keep them away from home longer than they expected.

It was afternoon before they were able to get away, and all through the lunch hour they were in a constant state of apprehension lest Aunt Gertrude prevail upon their mother to withdraw her permission for the journey.

"They'll never come back alive, mark my words!" declared their aunt. "They'll be bitten by those snakes on Blacksnake Island, as sure as fate. Why, even grown-up men won't go on that island. It's a terrible place. I've read all about it."

"We're not planning to explore the island, Aunt Gertrude," Frank explained. "We're going to cruise around it and see if we can find any sign of the fellows."

"Cruise around it!" their aunt sniffed. "As if I don't know boys! You'll not be satisfied until you've tramped from one end of the island to the other. But go ahead. Go ahead. I wash my hands of the affair. If you want to commit suicide, it's your own lookout," and she swept from the room in great indignation.

Mrs. Hardy did not share her fears. She knew her sons well enough to realize that they would not run into needless dangers, and when she kissed them good-bye her only request was that they would not stay away any longer than was necessary.

The bay was calm when they started out, and the *Sleuth* was running, as Joe expressed it, "like a watch."

It was a beautiful summer afternoon and the cool breeze out on the water was in welcome relief to the sweltering heat of the city streets. Spray flicked into their faces as the motorboat raced along toward the eastern gap. When they passed out of Barmet Bay and reached the open sea Frank headed the boat down the coast in the direction of Blacksnake Island.

"It isn't far from the coast. There's a channel of a little over a mile," he said to his brother. "We won't be able to make it to-night, but we'll stop over at Rock Harbor and go on again in the morning. By that time, Tony and the others shouldn't be far behind."

Toward the end of the afternoon they were in sight of Rock Harbor, a small port, where they spied a schooner at anchor in the distance. Rock Harbor was not a shipping point of great importance, but there were always a number of miscellaneous craft in evidence.

To enter the harbor they were obliged to pass within a short distance of the schooner, swinging about beneath the bows of the vessel.

As the *Sleuth* plunged through the water, in the very shadow of the ship, Joe suddenly gave an exclamation of surprise.

"Frank! Look up on deck—quick!"

Frank glanced hurriedly upward. He was just in time to see the figure of a boy moving away from the rail, but there was something familiar about the young fellow that made him look incredulously at his brother.

"Chet!"

"I'm sure it's him," returned Joe hurriedly. "I didn't get a very good look at his face, because he only looked over the rail and then he drew back—but I'm almost positive it was Chet!"

"But what on earth can he be doing on that schooner?"

"Probably he's a prisoner. Let's give him a hail."

They shouted the name of their chum half a dozen times, but their only response was from a villainous looking sailor who glared over the side at them and bade them get away from the ship.

"No use causing trouble," said Frank, in a low voice. "We'll go now, but we'll come back later."

He steered the motorboat away from the vicinity of the schooner, but instead of going on into the harbor he put out to sea again.

"It won't be long until it gets darker. Then we'll go back. If Chet is on that ship we'll get word to him somehow."

"Well, if it isn't Chet Morton it's his double," declared Joe. "Even if I didn't get a very good look at him, I know he was just about the same height and build and the same general appearance. What puzzles me is why he didn't call out to us. And why did he draw back from the rail in such a hurry?"

"He mightn't have had time to call to us. Perhaps he managed to escape just for a minute or so and they dragged him back before he could give a shout."

"There's something in that. And of course he mightn't have recognized us."

"He would have recognized the boat, I'm sure."

"There's something queer about it. If we come back later on we may be able to see him again. Did you notice the name of the schooner?"

"Yes," answered Frank. "I watched for it. The *Persis*. I think what we'd better do is this: We'll go back down the coast and loaf around until it gets darker. Then we'll come back to the harbor and try to come up to the schooner quietly. If there's a rope ladder handy I'll go up over the side and see what I can find out."

"It looks like our only chance. You'll have to go easy. If Chet and Biff are held prisoners on that ship they'll be well guarded. You might be captured yourself."

"That's where you will come in. If you hear sounds of a struggle or if I don't come back, go right into the harbor and notify the police so they can have the schooner searched."

Joe nodded. "All right. I'll keep watch."

Frank steered the motorboat back along the coast again and for the next hour or more they cruised about, waiting for twilight. At length sunset came and gradually the shadows fell. Lights began to twinkle in the town. Lights glowed from the mysterious schooner, now but a rakish shadow at the entrance to the harbor. When the lads judged that it was sufficiently dark to cover their approach, they returned, then crept quietly up on the ship.

They drew up close to the schooner's stern without being noticed and to Frank's relief he saw that a rope was dangling over the side. From the boat he reached out and seized it. The rope held fast; it supported his weight.

There were vague sounds from the deck above. The shuffling of feet. A burst of laughter from forward. Most of the men, he judged, would be in port, but it behooved him to move with caution.

"All set," he whispered to Joe.

"Right."

Frank swung himself away from the motor boat and began to climb slowly to the deck Water lapped against the schooner's hull. The night was very quiet. Complete darkness had fallen by now. In a few moments Joe could only distinguish his brother as an obscure shadow as he clambered slowly upward.

Anxiously, Joe Hardy watched. He saw his brother climb higher and higher until at last his head and shoulders were silhouetted above the side of the ship.

Then Frank scrambled quietly over onto the deck. He had removed his shoes so as to proceed with a minimum of sound, so that once he had disappeared over the side Joe could hear nothing. He crouched in the boat, waiting.

Finally he heard a low whistle from the deck above. He looked up. He could see Frank leaning over the side. His brother's face was only a grey blur. He motioned with his arm, indicating that Joe was to follow him.

The motorboat had been tied fast so, although Joe was somewhat puzzled, he was nothing loath to share the adventure. Seizing the rope, he swung himself free of the motorboat, then began to climb nimbly toward the deck.

The rope cut into his hands and the climb taxed his strength, but in a few minutes he

was near the top. Frank had moved back
from the side into the darkness again.

He scrambled over the side and dropped
lightly onto the deck. Frank was crouched in
the shadows waiting for him.

And at that moment a heavy hand fell on his
shoulder and a gruff voice said in his ear:

"All right, young fellow. Now we've got
you both!"

CHAPTER XI

THE ISLAND

JOE HARDY started violently. Then, realizing that he had been trapped, he dropped flat on the deck, wriggling to one side, wresting himself free of the clutching hand. He heard the man who had seized him give an angry grunt, then he saw the man lunging at him from the shadows. He dodged the outstretched arm and rolled over and over on the deck.

"Grab him, Mike!" roared another voice from near by, and then Joe was dimly aware that another struggle had started near the rail. He leaped to his feet and raced along the deck, the sailor in pursuit.

"Over the side, Joe!" shouted a voice that he recognized as being that of his brother.

He fled, hearing the pounding of feet on the deck close behind him. A dark figure stepped out of the shadows immediately ahead.

"Collar him!" roared the man at his back. The dark figure advanced with outstretched arms. Joe stepped neatly aside, dodged as the man swooped at him and blundered to the left. The two men collided violently, and by the time they had disengaged themselves Joe was a good five yards away.

The schooner was in an uproar.

A revolver roared from the shadows and the darkness was cleft by a crimson splash.

"Harbor thieves!" yelled a voice from behind. "Catch 'em!"

Footsteps pounded on the deck. Shouts and muttered imprecations rang out. A light flared from somewhere ahead. Out of the shadows rose a man who lunged fiercely at Joe, grappled with him, and they fell to the deck together. Joe managed to wrench himself free and rolled to one side, scrambling to his feet.

He heard a splash near by and a shout. "Over the side!" he could hear Frank calling again. His brother's voice was far below and he knew that Frank must have dived from the rail.

He was not far from the side of the schooner, and he raced for the rail just as half a dozen figures came plunging out of the gloom, their heavy boots thudding tremendously on the deck. Again the revolver crashed out and again the tongue of crimson flame licked its way through the blackness. The bullet passed within a few inches of Joe's head, and he ducked instinctively.

He reached the rail. Desperately, he scrambled up. But just as he poised for the dive a great hand closed about his ankle and some one seized the back of his coat. He felt himself dragged back, but with his free foot he kicked out. The grasp of his pursuer relaxed and Joe heard him grunt from the impact. The man staggered back.

The moment he was free, Joe went over the side.

He struck the cold water of the bay with a splash and went far down into the depths. Then he found himself rising again and at last he bobbed up over the surface.

He did not know where the motorboat was, but he swam ahead, at the same time keeping a wary eye above. He could see dark figures silhouetted above the side of the vessel and he could hear voices.

"He's down there!" declared a gruff voice.

"I almost had him!" shouted another. "I grabbed him just as he was going over, but he kicked me in the jaw."

"How many were there?" asked another sailor.

"Two," declared the gruff voice. "Harbor thieves—both of 'em. Come sneakin' aboard, one at a time. I caught one of 'em peepin' down into the galley where the cabin boy was peelin' potatoes and I followed him till he went back to the side, so I figured he had the rest of his pals down below. I grabbed him and clapped my hand over his mouth and made him wave for 'em to come up. But there was only one come up and Bill here grabbed him, but he got away.''

''Both of 'em get away?''

''Yeah! I hope they drown.''

Then a thrill of fear ran through Joe as he heard one of the men say:

''Keep quiet! Listen! Don't you hear some one swimming down there?''

The voices died down. Joe could see the figures leaning over the side as the sailors intently peered down into the darkness. He ceased swimming to tread water quietly.

''Take a shot at him!'' advised some one.

Joe let himself sink beneath the surface and hardly had he gone beneath the waves than he heard the muffled report of a revolver and a splash near by. He swam beneath the water until his lungs were almost bursting. Then, when he could stand it no longer, he came to the surface again. He was deep in the shadow of the ship and he had left the sailors behind, still watching the place where he had gone down.

''I don't believe there was any one there,''

muttered one of the men in a disappointed tone.

"No, I guess they both got away," agreed another. "We scared 'em off, anyway."

"Did they steal anything?"

"No. They didn't have time. I nailed the first one before he'd been on the ship long. I guess he just went on ahead to see if everything was clear."

"Aw, I'm goin' to bed. As long as we scared 'm off—"

The voices died away.

Relieved, Joe swam on. In a few minutes he caught sight of a dark shape ahead. It was the motorboat.

Silently, he swam toward it until he had reached the side. A voice whispered:

"Is that you, Joe?"

"Yes."

Frank had already gained the boat. He now leaned over the side and grasped Joe's hand, helping his brother on board. Dripping wet, they both crouched in the boat.

"Lucky they didn't see the *Sleuth* tied down here," whispered Frank. "I've been waiting here for you. I thought sure they had you."

"It was a close call. They mistook us for harbor thieves, eh?"

"Yes."

"Did you see Chet?"

"It wasn't Chet after all."

"No?"

"It was the cabin boy. I peeped into the galley and there he was, peeling potatoes. But it was another fellow altogether. He looked like Chet. So I started back and I had just reached the side when a sailor grabbed me. He kept his hand over my mouth so I couldn't call out. Then he grabbed my arm and made me wave over the side."

"I thought you were motioning for me to come on up."

"It was a bad mess. Oh, well, we're out of it, if we can only get away from here quick enough. I think we'd better wait for a while until the excitement dies down."

The boys waited in the darkness. Gradually the schooner became silent once more. The sailors had evidently returned to the forecastle. At length Frank judged that they could escape without trouble.

Fortunately, the engine of the motorboat responded immediately, and although the noise of their departure was sufficient to arouse the ship, the *Sleuth* shot away into the gloom so swiftly that their escape was assured. When they were several hundred yards away they looked back and they could see the lights of lanterns moving about near the stern, but they knew that the sailors would not put out after them. Even if they had, the motorboat would not be overtaken.

They circled about in the bay for some time and eventually put back into the harbor for the night. At first they were afraid that the men on the schooner might have given word to the harbor police to be on the lookout for them but, as Frank said, their consciences were clear and they had no doubt of their ability to explain the situation satisfactorily.

However, they were not intercepted and, in Rock Harbor, they tied the motorboat up for the night, going to a near-by hotel, where a sleepy night clerk assigned them to a room.

Early next morning they were away again.

"Blacksnake Island isn't far away now," said Frank. "We should be there in a few hours at the most."

There was no sign of the other boys, but Frank and Joe decided that they would not wait, as the others would overtake them at the island or would meet them on their return. They had replenished their boat with oil and gasoline, they had again inspected their supply of provisions and were in every way in readiness for the last lap of their search.

It was mid-morning before they came within sight of Blacksnake Island. It lay not far from the coast, a low, lean, sinister stretch of swampy land, terminating in rocky bluffs on the seaward side. There was a dank, heavy growth of vegetation and the island seemed to steam in the summer heat.

"Ugly looking place, isn't it?" remarked Frank, as the motorboat sped on its way.

The craft drew closer to the island. There was no sign of life. As they came nearer the boys could distinguish the fetid swamp land facing the coast, the still, silent trees that seemed to droop beneath the scorching sun and they felt a qualm of repulsion. Blacksnake Island was not an inviting place. It lived up to its name. It was a fit abode for serpents— not for human beings.

When they were within half a mile of the island, they heard a vague but familiar sound.

"Motorboat!" exclaimed Frank.

They listened. They could hear the sound of a motorboat, apparently approaching from the far side of the island. Frank spun the wheel.

"We'll head down the channel. No use letting them think we're bound for the island," he said. "It's not likely to have anything to do with our search, but it's best to play safe."

The *Sleuth* changed its course, so that Blacksnake Island was now to one side, and the motorboat appeared to be heading on down the coast. The Hardy boys scanned the dark bank of land intently.

The other boat appeared in view at last. It emerged slowly around the lower point, poking its nose inquisitively out into the channel as though to assure itself that the way was clear. Then it picked up speed and came surging out toward the mainland. At that distance, Frank and Joe could not readily distinguish the features of the men in the craft, but they saw that there were two of them. Frank's eyes narrowed as he surveyed the boat.

"Seems to me I've seen it before," he remarked, picking up the binoculars. He raised them to his eyes and gazed long and earnestly at the speeding craft. Finally he handed the glasses to Joe. "What do you think?" he asked.

"Why, of course we've seen it before!" Joe exclaimed, after a brief inspection. "We saw that boat in Barmet Bay!"

Frank nodded.

"It's the same motorboat that chased us the afternoon of the storm!"

CHAPTER XII

Into the Cave

Frank Hardy bent over the wheel.

"I'm going closer," he said. "We'll make absolutely sure of this."

He altered the course of the boat so that it would intercept the other craft, at the speed they were going. Then he turned up his coat collar and drew his cap lower over his eyes.

"If it's the same boat and if the same men are in it, we should be safe enough as long as they don't recognize us. They saw us that day, but they've never seen the *Sleuth*. We'll get as close to them as we can."

But the other craft had increased its speed. It was a powerful boat and a high curl of foam now rose from its bows as it plunged through the waves in a rapid flight toward the mainland in the distance. The roar of the engine was borne to the boys' ears on the breeze.

"We're going to lose them," muttered Frank. "They're too far ahead of us, unless we want to cut in and meet them right near the land."

103

"That will only make them suspicious."

"Yes, I guess we'd better let them go."

Still, he did not give up the attempt just then, opening the throttle so that the *Sleuth* was racing along at top speed. But the other boat had the advantage, and cut across their course with a quarter of a mile to spare. Joe gazed through the binoculars, striving to identify the two men.

"No use," he remarked, at last. "The fellow at the wheel is turned away from us, and the other man is bending down in the boat so I can't see his face."

"Is it the same boat?"

"I can't be positive. But I think so. It certainly looks very much like it."

"I'm almost sure. Of course, there might be lots of other motorboats just like it—but I've got a hunch that it's the same craft."

"What would it be doing at Blacksnake Island? There's no doubt that it came from there."

"That's for us to find out. We'll let them go on to the mainland. Then we'll circle back and go up the other side of the island."

In a short time the other craft disappeared from view, entering a small cove some distance down the coast, and Frank turned their boat about and headed toward Blacksnake Island again. They approached it from the seaward side and drew in as close to the island as they dared. The rocky bluffs were lonely and forbidding, seeming to offer no available landing place.

"We'll go right around it. If Chet and Biff are there we should be able to see their boat or a fire or some sign of them," said Frank, half questioningly, to his brother.

"After seeing that other motorboat, I'm pretty sure we won't see any sign of them at all. I'm pretty well satisfied that those men kidnapped them and brought them here. And if they did, you may be sure they'll be well hidden."

"We'll circle the island anyway, and if we don't see anything we'll land and make a search of the place."

But making a circuit of the island took longer than the boys expected. Blacksnake Island was bigger than it had first appeared. It was almost a mile in length, and correspondingly wide—a great, swampy tract of forbidding marsh at one end, rising to higher ground and desolate rocks at the other. On the swampy side there were sinister little creeks, dead bushes half inundated, logs floating about in the black water. Frank and Joe caught glimpses of triangular black heads forging slowly through the water here and there.

"The blacksnakes!" Frank exclaimed.

Once the motorboat passed within a few yards of one of these black reptiles. Fascinated, the boys watched the ugly black head that projected above the surface, and they could see the long, sinuous body writhing beneath the water as the snake swam toward the fetid marsh.

"There must be hundreds of them on that island."

"They're dangerous, too. I've read about them. A bite from one of them means your finish."

There were fewer snakes on the rocky side of the island and, after they had made the circuit without seeing any sign of human life, the boys decided to make a landing.

"Seeing that motorboat leaving here makes me believe some one is around," declared Frank. "I won't be satisfied until I find out for sure."

"We won't stay here all night?"

"It all depends. If we're satisfied that the island is deserted, we'll leave; but if we think we haven't searched thoroughly enough, we'll stay and hunt around again to-morrow. It'll take a few hours to give the place a thorough going-over."

"How about the snakes? Won't it be dangerous staying here all night?"

"Oh, we'll find some place where they can't

get at us. If the worst comes to the worst we can anchor the boat and stay in it.''

This decided, after some search they discovered a small cove, well protected from the sea, that appeared to offer a good landing place. The cove had a narrow entrance between the rocks, but widened out into a small lagoon, with water deep enough to enable the boys to bring their boat up close to a wide shelf of rock. They anchored the *Sleuth* then clambered up onto the rock.

''Feels good to stand on solid footing again,'' Joe commented.

''I'll say it does. Well, let's be starting. Which way shall we go? Is it to be north or south?''

''It doesn't matter much. To start with, we'll nose around among these rocks for a while.''

The sun blazed on the bare crags as the boys picked their way over the rocks and boulders. Away in the interior they could see the waving tops of trees in the steaming marsh, but for the time being they contented themselves with exploring the rocky end of the island. It was quite barren and it appeared that no human being had ever set foot upon the place.

''You can't blame them, either,'' said Frank, when Joe had remarked on this fact. ''It's certainly not a place where I'd care to build my happy home.''

After about an hour of desultory search they came upon something that proved conclusively that human beings had indeed been there before them—and not long previously, at that. Charred embers and a crude fireplace built of rocks in a little hollow told the boys that some-one had preceded them.

''We're on the track of something,'' declared Frank, as he examined the remains of the fire. ''This blaze was built here not long ago. Some one has camped here.'' He circled the rock, which dipped toward a patch of undergrowth and luxuriant grass. ''And here's a trail!'' he exclaimed.

It was merely a faint depression in the deep grass, but it proved that more than one person had passed that way before. The trail wound along through the verdure, away from the shore, leading toward the interior of the island.

''Well, if some one else has gone this way, we can follow the path, too,'' Joe remarked. ''Got your gun?''

''Yes.'' Frank patted his hip. Both boys had provided themselves with revolvers before leaving home. They were not adept with fire-arms, but the nature of their mission had prompted them to come prepared for any emergency. Fenton Hardy had a collection of weapons in his study, all trophies of his various cases, and the Hardy boys had each taken a small and efficient-looking automatic pistol for protection.

They struck out along the faint trail, the grass rustling about their feet. The green thicket loomed ominously before them and the heat became more intense.

Frank was striding along in advance, gazing at the thicket ahead, when he suddenly came aware of a disturbance in the grass almost at his feet. Some sixth sense warned him of danger. That strange tickling of the spine, man's instinctive reaction to the presence of a hidden peril, made him look down.

Immediately in front of him lay a huge blacksnake!

The reptile was easily five feet in length, and as the boy leaped back he could hear a prolonged hissing. The snake writhed and twisted, and its head came into view from amid the grass, the red tongue flickering wickedly.

Frank saw that the snake was coming directly at him. He leaped to one side, at the same time snatching his automatic from his hip pocket. He had not time to aim, but he pressed the trigger and pumped two shots in the direction of the reptile.

The snake stopped dead, then swiftly began to coil itself up in readiness to strike.

Not a word had been spoken. Frank had blundered back against Joe, who was unaware of the cause of his brother's sudden alarm. He quickly grasped the situation, however, and looked about him.

Close at hand, almost hidden by the grass, was a heavy stick. He bent and quickly snatched it up.

"Quick!" said Frank, taking it from him.

He brandished the stick and brought it down with terrific force upon the snake. The first blow did not kill the reptile, although it rendered it helpless. The hissing continued, the scarlet tongue flickered like flame. Then the boy brought the stick down again. It crushed in the evil black head. A few spasmodic wriggles, and the snake lay still.

"Whew!" breathed Frank, stepping back. "What a big brute he is!"

The boys inspected the reptile more closely, repressing a shiver of repulsion as they saw the sinuous, scaly body lying there in the grass.

"We'd better get away from here. Path or no path. Where there's one snake there are more. Its mate is probably close by."

The boys retreated until they gained the comparative safety of the rocks.

"It's lucky for me you saw that stick," declared Frank. "He was coming right for me, and the automatic wasn't much use. He was moving so quickly I couldn't have shot him. He was stirred up and angry, too. I guess I must have disturbed his morning nap.''

''We'll stick to the rocks for a while, I guess. It's time enough to go nosing around the interior when we've finished with the outside of the island.''

The boys descended a rocky slope that led into a small bay protected from the sea by a black reef. There were no snakes in sight as they skirted the shore, and then they came upon a well-beaten path leading up the side of a cliff.

''By the look of this path, the island isn't as deserted as it looks,'' Frank commented. ''Perhaps we'll have better luck following it.''

The path wound about among the rocks, seemingly in an aimless fashion, now diverging toward the shore, now bringing them farther inland. They followed it doggedly, however, convinced that it must have an ending somewhere, and that the termination would give them some clue as to the people who had used the trail before.

The trail at length brought them in front of a huge black opening in the rocks. It was a cave, over twelve feet in height, dark, gloomy and forbidding.

''Now what?'' asked Joe.

Frank glanced at his brother.

"Shall we go in?"

"You can't scare me. If you'll go, I'll go."

"The trail leads here. Other people must have gone in here. If they can do it, so can we."

"Lead on!"

Frank picked up a heavy stick lying among the rocks near the entrance to the cave. "You never know when we'll run into snakes around here," he remarked. "It's just as well to be ready for them."

Joe hunted around until he, too, found a club that would be serviceable in the event of their encountering more of the reptiles. He patted his hip to make sure that the automatic was still in his pocket.

"All set?"

"All set."

Frank stepped forward and entered the mouth of the cave. Joe followed at his heels.

For several yards the cave was illuminated by the light from outside, but as they went on the gloom became deeper until at length they were faced by impenetrable darkness. Frank had brought with him a pocket flashlight and he switched it on. A wide ring of light shone before them, showing the damp rock walls ahead.

They stepped forward cautiously. The floor of the cave sloped upward, but the great opening in the rock was of such extent that the ceiling was scarcely visible above in the light of the flash.

"I don't know where we're going, but we're on our way," said Frank, as they toiled on up over the rough rocks. His voice awakened tumultuous echoes that were flung back and forth from the massive walls.

The flashlight showed him at length a place where the floor dipped abruptly to a steep slope, although there was still a wide ledge at the top, sufficiently wide for them to proceed. He turned the light down the slope but could see nothing save inky blackness.

The boys proceeded slowly along the ledge.

There were numerous pebbles and small rocks underfoot. It was difficult to see these, because Frank was obliged to keep the flashlight centered on the trail ahead, and they were obliged to proceed cautiously in order to keep their footing. This circumstance led to disaster.

Unwittingly, Frank stepped on a small rock that rolled suddenly beneath his foot. He staggered, stepped on another rock that slipped to one side and then he sprawled forward, the flashlight spinning from his hand.

The light clattered among the rocks ahead and darkness fell about them.

"What's the matter?" asked Joe, alarmed.

"It's all right. I just slipped." Frank got to his feet. "I lost the light. It fell down here somewhere. Hang onto the back of my coat and I'll go ahead and get it."

Joe caught at the back of his coat and Frank slowly felt his way forward in the deep blackness.

Suddenly he lurched ahead, his feet sinking in a treacherous mass of sand and gravel. Wildly, he strove to retain his footing, but the effort was in vain. He felt himself slipping and, as he uttered an instinctive cry of warning to Joe, he was flung into space.

Joe, who had been clinging to Frank's coat, was wrenched to one side. He stepped forward, grasping for his brother, then he, too, went hurtling into the darkness.

They pitched down amid a clattering of rocks and pebbles. Then, with an icy shock, they plunged into a deep pool of water!

CHAPTER XIII

The Four Men

PROFOUND darkness enveloped the Hardy boys.

The blackness of the icy pool was no blacker than the darkness of the air above.

Frank rose spluttering to the surface, unharmed by his fall, and as he splashed about, his first thought was for his brother.

"Joe!" he shouted. "Joe!"

There was no answer except from the echoes, and the rocks shouted mockingly back at him. "Joe. . . . Joe. . . . Joe. . . ." growing fainter and fainter until they died away to a mere whisper.

Then there was a splashing almost at his side, as his brother rose to the surface of the pool and struck out blindly.

"Are you all right?" called Frank.

"I'm all right!" gasped Joe.

"Keep beside me. We'll try to find the edge of this pool."

Frank swam forward, groping ahead, until

115

at length his fingers touched the smooth rock at the water's edge. But the rock was almost vertical and it was so smooth and slippery that there was no hope of a handhold. He swam to one side, feeling the rock as he went. Despair seized him as he found that the rock still rose steeply above. If they had fallen into a circular pit they were doomed.

In pitch darkness, then, they battled their way about the border of the pool until at length Frank's searching fingers closed about a rocky projection that seemed to indicate a change in the surface of the cliff.

He was right. There was a small ledge at this point, and he was able to drag himself up on it. There was room enough for both of them, and he turned and grasped Joe's hand, dragging him up on the rock after him. They crouched there in dripping clothes, breathing heavily after their exertion. Presently Frank began to grope upward, still examining the surface of the cliff.

He found that it sloped gradually, and that the surface was rough, with a number of footholds.

"I think we can climb it," he told Joe. "It's mighty dark, but if we can ever get back on the main ledge again we'll be all right." He said this because he judged that the place that they had found was on the side of the pool that lay toward the entrance of the cave. If they had emerged on the other side and had regained the ledge they would have been in another dilemma, because they might not have been able to cross the treacherous breach in the trail that had proved Frank's downfall.

Frank groped his way up the face of the slope. He dug his foot against the first ledge and raised himself, clutching at a projection in the rock above. Then, scrambling for a further foothold, he managed to draw himself up. Here the slope became even more gradual and by pressing himself close against the rock, he was able to crawl on up, until at length he came to a flat shelf of rock that he recognized as the main ledge that they had followed from the entrance to the cave.

"I'm up!" he shouted back to Joe, and then he heard a scraping on the rocks, as his brother also began the ascent.

Joe made the climb without difficulty and in a short time rejoined his brother on the ledge.

"I guess we'd better go back," Frank said. "This cave seems to lead to nothing but trouble. We're better off out in the open."

"Is the flashlight lost?"

"Yes. I think it smashed when it fell against the rocks. Anyway, I'm not going back to look for it in the dark. That ledge was treacherous enough even when we had the light."

Step by step, proceeding cautiously, the Hardy boys made their way back toward the entrance to the cave. Their return journey was not so precarious because the entrance to the cave shone before them as a vague gray light and guided them on their way.

They reached the entrance at last and again stepped out into the bright sunlight. At first they were dazzled, after the blackness of the cave.

"First of all, we're going to dry our clothes," declared Frank, as he hunted around among the rocks for sticks that might serve for firewood. "I'm soaking wet."

"Me too. Thank goodness, it's warm out here."

"I'm glad I carried the matches in this waterproof case, or we'd have been out of luck."

They managed to find enough sticks and dry leaves to enable them to start a fire and soon they were standing about in various stages of undress, drying their soaked garments before the blaze. This occupied some time and it was mid-afternoon before they were able to proceed. They had taken some sandwiches with them from the boat and they made a lunch of these while their clothes were drying so that eventually, when they donned their garments again, they were warm, fed and contented.

"Where do we go from here?" inquired Joe.

"Anywhere but into caves," his brother replied. "I think we might as well follow along the shore again. One thing is certain—there have been people on this island, and not long ago at that. Why—"

Suddenly he stopped.

"Listen."

They remained quiet. Frank had heard what seemed to him like a distant shout, and as they listened he heard it again. It was a faint call that echoed among the rocks far ahead of them.

The boys looked at one another. Frank pressed his fingers against his lips as a caution to remain silent. Then, from among the rocks above them they heard another shout, clearer this time, evidently in response to the one they had first heard. The first shout was again repeated; then silence fell.

"That proves it," said Frank quietly. "There *are* people on this island."

"They're calling to each other."

"Sounded like that."

"We'll head down in the direction of the place that first shout came from. It was some one calling to some one else back up here among the rocks."

They went on in the direction from which the first call had been heard. For over ten minutes they proceeded carefully among the rocks until finally Frank caught sight of a curling column of smoke against the sky.

"Campfire," he said.

To approach this fire it was necessary for them to change their course and go up through the shrubbery toward higher ground. They moved slowly because they did not want to be seen until they had ascertained whether the strangers were friends or foes—and they were strongly suspicious that it might prove to be the latter.

A moving object ahead caught Frank's eye and he crouched down in the bushes, motioning to Joe. They peeped through the undergrowth and before them they could see a flat surface of rock in the center of which a fire had been built. Three men were about the fire. Two of these were sprawled in the grass at the verge of the rock while one was standing beside the fire stirring the contents of a pot that hung from a tripod above the blaze. It was this man that had first caught Frank's eye.

The strangers had not noticed the Hardy boys' approach.

"We'll crawl up closer," whispered Joe.

Frank nodded.

They began to make their way quietly forward through the bushes. Frank, who was in the lead, kept a wary eye for snakes and also kept watching the three men about the fire. The boys' approach demanded the utmost caution.

Foot by foot they made their way closer to the trio about the blaze until at last they were so close that they could distinguish what the men were saying. Also, they could distinguish the faces of the speakers.

They were the three men who had been in the motorboat the day of the storm in Barmet Bay!

Although the boys had expected this, they could scarcely restrain murmurs of astonishment. This proved definitely that the motorboat they had seen that morning was the same motorboat that had followed them in Barmet Bay.

The boys listened.

"No answer to that letter yet, is there?" one man was asking.

The fellow by the fire shook his head.

"No answer yet. Oh, well, we can wait."

"We can't wait forever," grumbled the other. "I'm not keen on staying on this confounded island much longer.

"There's lots worse places," remarked the man at his side significantly.

"What do you mean?"

"Jail."

"Oh, I suppose so. But I wish this business

would get cleared up. I want to get back to the city and have a good time."

"We all want to get back. But there's no use rushing things," said the man standing by the fire. "We'll be well paid for our waiting."

"Do you think we've made a mistake? I tell you, it's been worrying me. If we've gummed up this job by doing a trick like that I'll never forgive myself."

"No—there's no mistake. Don't worry about that," scoffed the man at the fire. "Didn't we look things over mighty careful-like before we started?"

"Yes," admitted the other slowly. "But they keep harpin' on that tune all the time and I'm beginnin' to think there may be somethin' in it."

"Where's Red?" demanded the third man. "Didn't you call him?"

"Yeah, I called him. This is him now. He's comin' down from the grove."

Suddenly Frank clutched his brother by the arm and flattened himself against the ground. A footstep sounded immediately behind them. Twigs crackled.

Unobserved, a man had approached to within a few feet back of them, striding silently through the deep grass.

The boys remained motionless, wondering if they had been seen. For a breathless second they lay rigid in the bushes, then the footsteps passed by within a few inches of Frank's outstretched hand. They heard his deep voice:

"When did you all get back?"

"Just a few minutes ago," replied the man at the fire. "We left the boat in the bay. Anything new?"

"Nothing new," growled the deep voice. "The prisoners are still safe and sound." One of the other men chuckled.

"Have they quieted down yet?"

"No!" growled the newcomer. "They kicked up a big fuss all the time you were away. Still keep sayin' we've made a mistake."

"Mistake, nothin'!" the man by the fire declared. "There's been no mistake about this job! They can't fool me!"

CHAPTER XIV

The Storm

The four men had dinner about the campfire and when the meal was over the man they called Red got up.

"May as well go back to the cave," he remarked. "It's cooler than out here."

"It's hot enough to put a man to sleep out on these rocks," said one of the others. "Yeah, let's go on up to the cave."

"I don't like the idea of stayin' too close to the cave," growled the man who had been by the fire. "If anybody comes around here and should find us they'll have to look some to find *them* as long as we're not near the cave, see?"

"That's all right, Pete," retorted Red. "If any one comes on this island we'll know of it in lots of time to clear away from the cave. We may as well keep cool."

There was a grumbled assent from Pete, and then the Hardy boys heard sounds of receding footsteps as the quartette strode off through the grass. They waited until the men were out of earshot, then peered through the undergrowth.

"Shall we follow them?" asked Joe eagerly.

"You bet we will! I want to know where this cave is that they're talking about. And I want to know who the prisoners are that they mentioned."

"Do you think it really could be Chet and Biff?"

"I'm almost sure it is. Didn't you hear the fellow saying that the prisoners kept insisting that there'd been a mistake? We've figured it out right all along. They captured Chet and Biff in mistake for us."

The Hardy boys began moving through the undergrowth on the trail of the four men. They crouched down and kept to the shelter of the bushes so that they were able to proceed at a good rate of speed without exposing themselves to view.

"If we can only get into the cave and get Chet and Biff free!" exclaimed Joe.

"It won't be any too easy. They seem to be guarding them pretty closely. First of all, we've got to be certain that it's them."

"I don't think there's any doubt of that. Everything hangs together too well. If we could get them out we could run for the boat and get them away to the mainland."

"That's what we'll have to plan on. But the main thing is to find this cave."

"Yes, of course."

The four men in the lead had entered the outskirts of a small grove toward the center of the island. Frank could just see the head and shoulders of the last man disappearing into the woods. He marked the spot where the fellow had entered the grove and the Hardy boys made toward it. They found it comparatively easy to follow the trail, for the others had beaten down the grass and twigs in passing, and in a few minutes they had reached the grove.

"Go slow," cautioned Frank, as they entered the shadow of the trees. "They may have seen us crossing the clearing."

They listened for a moment. They could hear the crashing of branches and the crackling of twigs, the distant hum of voices, as the quartette continued through the woods, so they went ahead.

The wood was steaming hot and the ground was dank underfoot. The grass was long and the leaves of the trees drooped of their own weight. Once Frank saw a blacksnake scurrying away through the grass, but none of the serpents molested them. The path the boys followed was beaten down by the feet of the men ahead and they made easy progress until

at length the sight of a clearing ahead warned
them to again exercise caution.

They crept along through the trees and
underbrush until the clearing came fully into
view. It was at that part of the interior of
the island where the swamp gave way to the
rocks, and the grassy clearing led in a gradual
slope to a high wall of rock, at the base of
which was the mouth of a cave. As the Hardy
boys watched, they could see the four men at
the opening. One of the fellows, a tall, dark
man, was mopping his brow with a handkerchief, while another, a man with a shock of red
hair, was just going into the cavern. The other
two had flung themselves down on the rocks in
the shadow of some overhanging bushes.

"So that's the cave!" exclaimed Frank.

"I wonder if Chet and Biff are inside."

"Most likely. I wish we could get a little
closer."

"Too dangerous. They can see any one
coming into the clearing."

This was true. The cave had evidently been
chosen not only for its possibilities as a shelter but for its defensive virtues as well. It
was plainly the hangout of the gang.

"We'll have our work cut out for us to get
in there," muttered Frank. "The place is too
much in the open. Our only chance is to wait
until some of them go away."

"We might be able to sneak up closer when they're asleep."

"We'll try it. The only thing for us to do right now is wait until they're all asleep."

The boys settled themselves down in the bushes, prepared for a vigil until nightfall. It was now late in the afternoon, and when Frank glanced up at the sky he saw that clouds had gathered. The sunshine had gone, for a dense black cloud obscured the sun. The sultry and oppressive heat of the afternoon had evidently presaged a storm.

"Looks like rain."

"It sure does," agreed Joe, looking up.

As though in corroboration, there was an ominous rumble of thunder. The wind had died down. Every leaf, every blade of grass was still. The clouds were massing silently.

However, the storm held off, and although the sky was overcast and threatening, twilight fell without rain. Frank and Joe, from their hiding place in the bushes, watched the four men moving aimlessly about the cave that afternoon. Two of them had remained inside the cave for a long time while the other pair chatted on the rocks outside.

Night came at last. From the interior of the cave came the flicker of flames, and the Hardy boys knew that the gang was making a fire for the night.

The heat was still oppressive. Darkness fell without moon or stars.

"We'll soon be able to creep up on them now," said Frank. "If we can only get close enough to hear what they're saying we'll probably be able to make sure if they have Chet and Biff with them."

The boys waited until the fire had died down. The four men had all disappeared within the cave.

"Quiet, now," Frank whispered. He began to make his way out of the undergrowth. Joe followed close behind. They crept up toward the entrance to the cave.

They were about half-way across the open space when the whole scene about them was suddenly revealed with startling clarity in the livid glow of a flash of lightning. This was followed immediately by a crash of thunder that seemed to shake the very rocks on which they stood. As though this were but a prelude, rain began to fall, gently at first, then with increasing force. Other lightning flashes followed. Then the storm broke in all its fury.

A gradually rising wind began to rake the tree-tops and the swishing of leaves and creaking of limbs could be plainly heard. The dull booming of the waves on the distant shore, the moaning of the wind, the driving spatter of rain, the constant peals of thunder, continually rose in volume, and the rain poured furiously from the black skies above.

The storm had broken so suddenly that the Hardy boys were taken aback. Their first impulse was to race for the shelter of the cave, but second thought told them that this would be unwise, for the men in the cave might be aroused by the storm.

"We'd better go back to the boat," said Frank, turning about. "It's liable to be wrecked."

Joe had almost forgotten about their motorboat. It was on the seaward side of the island and the storm was coming in from the sea. Although the boat was partly protected by the little cove into which they had brought it, there was every danger that the storm might cast the craft up on the rocks and wreck it. The consequences, in that case, would be grave. They would be unable to escape from Blacksnake Island at all without giving themselves up to the gang.

The boys turned and fled back across the rocks. Rain streamed down upon them. Thunder crashed. Lightning flickered, illuminating for brief seconds the tossing trees and the tumbled rocks before them.

Joe, during the afternoon, had occupied himself ascertaining the position of the grove and the cave relative to the little bay in which they had left the motorboat and he had come to the conclusion that the grove was not far away from the end of the island and almost in a direct line with the cove. Now, in their mad race toward the shore, he took the lead, heading toward the rocky bluffs.

The Hardy boys stumbled through the grove, keeping somehow to the trail. They were aided by the lightning flashes that gave spasmodic illumination, revealing the soggy leaves, the black branches, the tossing tree-tops bowed in the wind.

The storm had become a din of furious sound. The gale shrieked its way across the island from the booming sea and the thunder rolled like a battery of cannon while the rain beat down on the forest in a drumming downpour.

The boys were soaked to the skin. They fled toward the shore, keeping their course more by instinct than judgment, and all the time there was the dread thought in their minds that they were lost if the *Sleuth* should be cast up on the rocks and wrecked.

CHAPTER XV

A STARTLING ANNOUNCEMENT

THE Hardy boys reached the cove in the nick of time. Although the place was protected from the full fury of the sea, the high wind had lashed the waves to such an extent that the boat was pitching and tossing about, in imminent danger of running aground.

The beach was sandy, however, and after some maneuvering, the boys were able to run the boat up on the shore, where it was safe enough. The storm by this time was showing some signs of abating, although the rain was still pouring in undiminished vigor. Frank rummaged about in the boat until he located their oilskins, and these they donned, although their clothes were already drenched.

"I'd hate to be out at sea on a night like this," shouted Frank, as the lightning revealed the tossing inferno of waves under the black skies.

At that moment a light flashed away out to the right.

"A boat!" exclaimed Joe.

"Heading toward the island!"

They kept their eyes fixed on the place where they had seen the light. In a few moments a vivid splash of lightning cut the darkness and they had a momentary glimpse of a small motorboat tossing about in the black waves.

"He'll never make the shore in this storm," said Frank, shaking his head.

"Can it be Tony?"

"I hardly think so. He wouldn't come close in such a storm."

"That's true, too."

"I think it's some outsider."

"Do you think we can help him?"

"I don't think so. He'll probably pile up on the rocks."

"Perhaps he's one of the gang."

"That's so," agreed Frank. "I hadn't thought of that. Perhaps he knows where he's going, after all. Still, it won't hurt to go down the shore a bit and see if he makes his landing all right."

They went on down the shore in the darkness, picking their way among the rocks, feeling in their faces the salt spray blown in from the sea. The dull booming of the surf and the howling of the wind provided an almost deafening cacophony of sound. Every little while, a lightning flash would reveal the little boat, slowly heading in toward the shore.

Suddenly Frank stopped short, grasping his brother by the arm.

"I saw a light ahead."

"I thought I did too. Right on the shore."

They waited. In a moment the light reappeared. It bobbed slowly up and down and appeared to be moving down toward the beach.

"Somebody is going down to meet the boat. It must be one of the gang," declared Frank.

The boys went forward more cautiously. The next flash of lightning showed that Frank's assumption was correct. They could see four men in oilskins trudging down among the rocks. The man in the lead carried a powerful electric lantern that cast a vivid beam of light upon the rain-washed boulders.

They saw that the man in the motorboat was heading toward a small bay that afforded ideal protection from the storm. The entrance was very narrow and great waves dashed over the rocks with showers of white spray, but the man in the boat guided his craft skillfully into the channel. He was in difficulties for a few moments, but by good steering brought the craft around. Then it shot forward, making the channel neatly, and surged down toward the beach.

The men in oilskins were there to meet him.

The boat was run up on the sand and the lone steersman sprang out and splashed through the water. For a few moments the five men conferred, standing there on the dark beach, with the wind whipping their oilskins about their legs, the lantern gleaming like a white eye, and the rain pouring down upon them. They looked like five sinister birds of prey as they stood there in the storm, and then they turned and began to walk back up over the rocks toward the center of the island.

"This must be their landing place," said Frank. "And that means they must have a good trail from here to the cave."

"Let's follow them," suggested Joe.

"Just what I was going to say. We know our boat is safe, and we can't get any wetter than we are now."

The boys therefore made their way down to the place where the five men had been standing. They could see the reflection of the lantern as it bobbed up and down while the quintette trudged back toward the trees, and they followed. True enough, there was a well-defined trail among the rocks and they made easy progress, considering the darkness and the fact that the trail was unknown to them.

The height of the storm had passed and the rain had settled down to a steady downpour. The roar of the thunder had diminished to an occasional distant rumble, and the lightning flashes were less frequent. The wind, too, had died down.

The light ahead guided them up the trail, across the rocks, then into the grove again, and in a short time they again emerged on the edge of the clearing and could see the dull mass of the granite slope before them. The fire still gleamed, and they could see the five men go into the cave, which was brilliantly illuminated for a moment in the light of the lantern which the first man held so that the others might pass.

"We may as well go right up," said Frank. "We've come this far. There isn't any use backing down now."

"I'm with you."

They crossed the rocks and crept up toward the entrance to the cave. They found tumbled boulders about the opening that afforded good protection and they were able to make their way up to within a few feet of the cave mouth without danger of being seen. The wind and the rain still created sufficient noise to drown out any sounds that they might have made in their approach.

Through an opening in the boulders, they peeped into the cave. As they were in darkness they knew there was little chance that they would be seen by the men within; as for the latter, they were in the full glare of the fire, which one of the men had replenished from a pile of wood near by. The boys, therefore, could see without being seen.

The men were divesting themselves of their oilskins, and one of them, the newcomer, had flung himself down on a pile of blankets, as though exhausted.

"I tell you it was a tough trip," he was saying. "I was sure I was going to be wrecked. I couldn't find the passage. If you hadn't come along with the lantern when you did I'd have been washed up on the rocks and the boat would have been smashed to pieces."

"Well, you're here, and that's all there is to it," declared the man they called Red. "You shouldn't have started out when you saw a storm was coming up."

"I didn't know it was going to be so bad. Anyway, I thought I'd get here before it broke."

"It must have been good news that brought you out here to-night," declared one of the others, sitting down.

"I'll say it was good news," said the newcomer. "Mighty good news."

"What is it?" they asked eagerly.

"I've found out why Fenton Hardy didn't pay any attention to that letter."

The boys listened eagerly. At the mention of their father they knew that all their sus-

picions had been verified. They waited tensely
as the conversation went on.

"Why?" asked Red.

"He didn't get it."

"Why didn't he get it?"

The newcomer paused and smiled.

"The reason he didn't get it," he said,
slowly and triumphantly, "is because we've
got him."

"Got him?"

"We've got Fenton Hardy!"

"How?"

"Where?"

"How do you know?"

Questions were fired at the newcomer from
all parts of the cave. He was enjoying the
sensation he had caused. As for the hidden
listeners, they experienced only a sickening
amazement.

"The gang got him in Chicago last night. I
just got word this afternoon. He went out
there to catch Baldy; but the boys got wind
of it and they laid a trap for him. He stepped
right into it."

"Good!" exclaimed the red-headed man, rubbing his hands. "What could be sweeter?
We've got Hardy and we've got his sons—"

"By the way, how are they acting?" asked
the newcomer.

"Oh, still kicking up a fuss—the young

brats," growled the man called Pete.   "They say they ain't the Hardy boys at all."

"Don't worry about that.   Bring 'em out here."

One of the men got up from beside the fire and disappeared into the rear of the cave.   His footsteps died away and the Hardy boys judged that there must be some sort of inner chamber to the place.   In a short time he returned, pushing ahead of him two boys.   Frank and Joe peered forward, striving to catch a glimpse of the lads' features.

With a clanking of chains, the boys emerged into the firelight.

They were Chet Morton and Biff Hooper!

The lads were handcuffed and their ankles were bound by a gleaming length of chain, just long enough to enable them to walk.   They appeared thin and tired, their shoulders drooped wearily, and as they stood before the fire they said nothing.

"Well, Hardys," said the red-haired man in a harsh voice, "we have some news for you."

"We've told you before," said Chet. "You've made a mistake.   We're not the Hardy boys."

The man named Pete stepped suddenly forward from the shadows and cuffed Chet savagely on the side of the head.

"Shut up!" he snarled, and cuffed Biff

Hooper as well. "No more of that. We're tired of listenin' to it. You're the Hardy boys, all right, and it won't do you no good to deny it."

"You've made a mistake!" insisted Chet stubbornly.

"We'll show you how much of a mistake we've made!" roared one of the men. "We brought you out here to tell you something. Our men have got your father at last."

"Mr. Hardy?" exclaimed Chet greatly taken aback.

"Yes, Mr. Hardy!" exclaimed Red, mimicking him. "That shot sunk home, didn't it? We've got him, and we've got you, and we'll starve you into making your mother come across with the money we want. If you have been holding out, hoping your father would come for you, it's no good now. We've got him and we've got you, so you may as well give up."

"There's no use asking us," declared Biff. "We're not the Hardy boys."

Red cuffed him viciously over the ears again. Biff staggered back from the blow.

"Oh, take them back and chain them up again," Red said, in disgust. "Let 'em starve for a while and they'll come around and tell the truth!"

"If I could get loose for about two minutes

I'd show you—,'' declared Biff, clenching his fists.

But the red-haired man only laughed contemptuously. The Hardy boys, from their hiding place, saw Pete come forward and drag Chet and Biff back into the darkness at the rear of the cave, their chains clanking as they went.

CHAPTER XVI

The Alarm

The Hardy boys were quivering with excitement. They had found the whereabouts of their chums; they had learned the dismaying news that Fenton Hardy had been captured by his enemies; they had discovered the hiding place of the gang. All this had taken place in a few fleeting hours.

Their first problem was to release Chet and Biff. But at first glance that seemed impossible. For when Pete came back into the cave he flung a bunch of keys into the sand beside the fire and laughed harshly.

"They'll get tired bein' chained up to a rock after a few more days," he said. "They'll come through yet."

"We can wait as long as they can," declared Red.

"If they'll only write a letter to their mother now and tell her we want that ransom we'll be sitting pretty. Fenton Hardy can't come after them—that's certain."

"Well, it's a good day's work. I'm goin' to sleep," said one of the other men. He pulled a blanket about him and curled up beside the fire.

"Good idea," remarked Red. "We might as well all turn in."

Shortly afterward, the various members of the gang were sprawled about in their blankets on the sand. Frank noticed that they all slept on the same side of the fire, and also noted that the reason for this was that on one side of the cave the floor was a ledge of rock.

"We'll wait till they go to sleep," he whispered to Joe.

His brother nodded. The two boys remained crouched among the rocks. The rain had died away to a mere drizzle.

Gradually the fire, untended, died down, and there was only a faint, rosy glow through the interior of the cave. Two or three of the men had talked together in low murmurs for a while, but gradually their voices died away and soon the boys could hear their snores. It was nearly an hour, however, before they were satisfied that all the men were asleep.

"I'm going in after Chet and Biff," whispered Frank, with determination.

"I'm with you."

"The keys are still lying beside the fire."

"Good."

Frank rose from his cramped position among the rocks. Joe followed his example. Quietly, they moved toward the entrance of the cave.

The snores of the slumbering men were unbroken. Frank took the lead and tiptoed slowly forward. Step by step, keeping a wary eye on the recumbent forms wrapped in the blankets, the boys made their way into the cave.

Frank remembered where the keys had been thrown, and now he saw them in the sand. The faint glow of the firelight gleamed on them.

The keys were on the side of the fire nearest the men. It would be a delicate job to get possession of them. He bent forward and crawled on hands and knees. Joe came silently behind.

Frank skirted the fire, then groped carefully forward.

There was a mutter from the shadows. One of the men stirred in his sleep.

The boys remained rigid.

The muttering died away. After a long pause, Frank again reached for the keys.

His hands closed over them. He gripped them tightly so that they would not jangle together. Then he moved slowly back onto the rock ledge, the keys safely in his grasp.

The Hardy boys continued their silent jour-

ney toward the darkness in the rear of the
cave. The dying fire cast little light.

Little by little they edged forward into the
depths of the cave, past the sleeping men. The
slightest noise, they knew, might be sufficient
to arouse one of the gang. They proceeded
with the utmost caution toward the back of the
cavern.

At length Frank found what he sought. It
was a dark patch in the rear wall—the entrance
to the inner chamber.

He reached it safely and groped his way
through into the pitchy blackness beyond. He
stopped and listened. The sound of deep
breathing told him that his two chums were
asleep within.

He reached back and laid a restraining hand
on Joe's arm, indicating that he was to remain
at the mouth of the inner chamber and keep
watch. Joe realized his intention and remained
where he was. Frank then continued.

Cautiously, he groped about in the darkness,
moving slowly forward. At length his hand
fell upon an outstretched arm, then a shoulder
which stirred slightly.

He bent forward and shook the sleeper.

"Chet!" he whispered.

The other boy moved and began to sit up.
The chains jangled.

"Quiet!" whispered Frank, fearing that his

chum might be alarmed at this sudden and surprising awakening and make some sound.

"Who is it?" whispered the other.

"It's me—Frank. I've come to help you get free."

From the darkness he heard a gasp of surprise, but it was quickly silenced.

"I'll waken Biff," replied Chet. Frank had merely guessed at this being Chet Morton whom he had awakened, and found that his guess had been correct.

In a few minutes Biff had been aroused.

"The men are asleep," whispered Frank. "Don't ask questions. Keep quiet until we get outside. I have the keys. Where is the lock?"

"We're chained to the rock," Chet whispered in return. He grasped Frank's hand, guiding it to the wall of the cave until his fingers closed on a heavy padlock. "There you are!"

Frank tried several keys before he found the one that fitted, but at length the padlock snapped open. He grasped the chain with his other hand so that it did not fall to the floor with a clatter. He lowered it gently.

"Now for the handcuffs."

Chet extended his wrists and Frank finally located the small key that opened the handcuffs. He removed them, then released Chet's feet in a similar manner. Then he crawled over to Biff, releasing him from his chains.

All this work had been done with a minimum of noise, and as there had been no warning whisper from Joe, they assumed that the men in the outer cave had not been aroused.

Frank led the way out, the three crawling on hands and knees into the main cave. They could see Joe crawling ahead of them, past the ruby glow of the embers.

The snores of the men continued without interruption. Frank was jubilant. The most dangerous part of the affair was over. Could they but gain the entrance in safety and reach their motorboat in the cove before the gang should discover that their prisoners had escaped, all would be well.

Frank caught sight of a flashlight lying in the sand. His own light had been lost in the rock cave the previous day and he knew they would need a light to regain their boat.

He reached carefully over for it. His hands closed about the black cylinder and the light was his.

Chet and Biff nodded appreciatively when they saw what he had done. The flashlight would be a big factor in aiding their escape.

Joe had reached the entrance to the cave by now. They saw him get to his feet and glide silently out into the darkness.

Frank reached the end of the ledge. The flashlight was clutched in his hand. Slowly he rose to his feet. But a small pebble betrayed him. He lost his balance and staggered for a second.

Had it not been for the flashlight the emergency would have passed because he flung out his hand and supported himself against the wall of the cave. But the heavy flashlight struck a loose projection of rock.

There was a grinding clatter of stone as the rock came free.

In the dead silence of the cave the noise seemed magnified many times. Frank knew that the sleepers would be aroused. He threw caution to the winds.

He leaped forward, gaining the entrance at a bound. Chet Morton and Biff Hooper, seeing that nothing was to be gained by further caution, scrambled to their feet and raced in pursuit.

The noise of the dislodged rock had already wakened one of the men. He raised himself on elbow in alarm and peered about. Then he saw the fleeing figures in the mouth of the cave and heard the running footsteps.

He sprang at once to his feet.

"They're getting away!" he roared. "Wake up, men! They're getting away!"

Instantly pandemonium prevailed within the

cave. The men hastily tumbled out of their blankets, bewildered at being aroused from slumber.

The Hardy boys and their chums, racing across the rocky stretch on the outskirts of the cave, heard the uproar and the cry:

"After them! Don't let them escape!"

CHAPTER XVII

CAPTURE

THE men in the cave lost no time in taking up the pursuit. They had been sleeping in their clothes and, once aroused, hurried out of the cave in search of the fugitives.

The boys raced across the rocks. Behind them they could hear shouts as the gangsters called to each other. Then came the crash of a revolver as one of the men pumped shot after shot in their direction.

Biff sprawled full length on the rocks.

"Are you hurt?" asked Joe, stopping to help him rise.

"No, I'm all right," gasped Biff, scrambling to his feet. He had suffered bruises but seemed otherwise uninjured. However, when he began to run again Joe noticed that he was limping and his progress was slower than formerly.

Frank had the battered flashlight, but he did not dare switch it on for fear of revealing their whereabouts to the men. The latter, however, were stumbling along behind, following the

trail by reason of the noise the boys made in
their mad flight toward the trees.

The men had the advantage in that they
knew every inch of the rocky ground. The
boys had to proceed more cautiously because
it was unfamiliar to them, especially to Chet
and Biff.

Biff was limping along in the rear and Joe
purposely slowed down his pace so as to remain with his chum. But the delay was fatal.
Out of the darkness came one of their pursuers,
and with a growl of triumph he flung himself
at Biff.

His arms encircled the lad's legs in a perfect
tackle and Biff went down with a crash. Joe
wheeled about and plunged upon them, strik-
ing out desperately to fight off Biff's attacker.
They struggled fiercely in the darkness. Joe
felt his fist crash into the man's face and he
heard a grunt of pain. Biff was wriggling out
of his assailant's grasp, and the boys might
indeed have made their escape had it not been
that the other men came running up out of the
shadows.

With a roar of fury, two of them plunged at
the boys and hauled them away from their
comrade.

"After the other two!" shouted a voice,
which they recognized as that of Red,
"They're heading for the bushes!"

Joe and Biff found themselves roughly hauled to their feet, their arms held tightly behind them. They heard the clatter of footsteps as two of the other men ran after Frank and Chet.

"Back to the cave with 'em," growled Red. "Looks like we've got one of the guys that helped 'em get away. I've been thinkin' all day that there was some one hangin' around here that we didn't know about."

The lads were shoved and pushed ahead of their captors, dragged and bundled across the rocks until they reached the cave. Then they were roughly shoved through the entrance into the light of the fire.

"Ah! I thought so!" declared Red. "One of the guys that tried to help them get away." He peered closer at Joe. "Blessed if it ain't one of those two boys that was in the boat with the Hardys that day."

One of the other men ordered the boys to sit down, and they crouched beside the stirred-up fire, sick at heart, wondering how it fared with Frank and Chet.

When Joe and Biff were captured it was Chet's first impulse to turn and go back, but a warning shout from Frank restrained him.

"Keep running!" he called. "If they're caught we'll have a chance to get help."

The wisdom of this course flashed through

Chet's mind at once. If they went to the aid
of their comrades they would probably all be
captured and in a worse position than before.
But if two, or even one, managed to escape, it
would be possible to bring help to the island
and effect the release of the others.

Chet heard Frank crash into the undergrowth. It was pitch dark, and although he
tried to follow he knew he had left the trail.
He did not call out because he was afraid of revealing his whereabouts to the men behind,
but he blundered on, hoping to catch up with
Frank. As for the latter, he was quite unaware of Chet's predicament.

Chet crashed into the bushes. Branches
whipped his face. Roots gripped his feet.
He struggled on through the dense growth,
blindly, in the darkness. Far ahead of him he
could hear Frank making his way through the
underbrush, but when he tried to go toward
the sound he found that his sense of direction
was confused.

He struggled on for some time. Suddenly he
saw a patch of gray light ahead. It was the
open sky and he soon plunged out of the undergrowth into a rocky clearing. He breathed a
sigh of relief.

But the relief was short-lived.

A dark figure loomed up before him. He
dodged swiftly to one side, but a huge hand

caught at his clothing. He was spun violently around and then he was caught by the collar, despite his struggles.

"Got you!" grunted the dark figure, with satisfaction. "Now if we can only get the other—"

He said no more, but shoved Chet before him across the rocks. Then it was that Chet found that, instead of fleeing farther away from the cave he had really made a circle in the wood and had emerged directly into the clearing again. He was sick with disappointment. He wriggled and twisted in the grasp of his captor, but the man was too strong for him and he shook Chet vigorously, tripping his feet from under him.

"None of that! You come along with me!" he rasped.

And in a few minutes Chet was shoved back into the cave, where he found Biff Hooper and Joe Hardy crouched silently beside the fire, with downcast faces.

Frank alone had escaped.

Frank knew that Chet had got lost but he did not dare call out, for he could also hear the running tramp of feet that told him their pursuers had not yet given up the chase. If he could only reach the cove and get the motorboat started he would be able to go over to the mainland for help. If only one escaped, it would be sufficient to save the others. He could not afford to risk his own capture in seeking Chet.

He crashed on through the bushes, trying to make as little noise as possible. But he was off the trail, and the tangled undergrowth was growing denser with every forward step he took.

He still clutched the flashlight that had been the cause of their undoing. He was glad he had found it, because in the pitch blackness he was unable to find his way. He could hear the roar of the waves, but they appeared to come from all sides and he was unable to judge accurately the route to the shore.

Frank decided that he would not make use of the flashlight until it was absolutely necessary. There was too much danger that its gleam might be seen by one of the searchers. And he knew that the gang would not give up the chase as long as they knew he was on the island.

"Perhaps they don't know there are two of us," he thought. "If Joe can convince them that he rescued Chet and Biff single-handed they won't know about me and they won't keep on searching."

In this lay his only hope—in this and in the chance that he would be able to reach the motorboat and make his escape before being seen. But if the gangsters knew he was still free they would leave no stone unturned to find him, as they would know that if he once left the island they were lost.

He blundered about in the deep thicket, turning vainly this way and that. Great vines trailed across his face; he brushed aside stubborn branches and soggy wet leaves; he stumbled over roots and little bushes; the deep grass rustled and hissed at his feet.

There was no other way. He would have to use the flashlight. The darkness was impenetrable. Trees and bushes enclosed him. He could not see where he was going.

He switched on the light and, to one side of him, descried a sort of passage among the bushes, so he headed in that direction. He managed to get free of the worst of the vines and the thick foliage and found himself in a forest aisle. He went down it, in the direction of the booming surf. His heart beat quickly at the thought that he was now free and that he would soon be back at the boat. What had happened to Chet? He judged that his chum was either captured now or lost in the grove. Frank knew that he could not wait to learn Chet's fate because any delay would be fatal to them all.

He had switched out the flashlight and was plunging along through the darkness when the forest aisle suddenly took a twist and he found

himself again floundering in the midst of trees
and trailing vines that entangled him.

Frank switched on the flashlight again.

And a second later he heard a grim voice
from close by:

"Throw up your hands!"

He wheeled about and found himself suddenly bathed in a ring of light. Some one
was standing only a few feet away with a
flashlight leveled at him, and in the beam of
the flashlight he could see a glittering revolver
aimed directly toward him.

"Throw up your hands!" rasped the voice
again, "or you'll be shot."

Slowly Frank raised his hands above his
head.

"That's better. Now march back ahead of
me. Back to the cave, young fellow. We've
got you all now. Forward march!"

CHAPTER XVIII

BACK TO THE CAVE

"THIS is a piece of luck!" declared the red-headed man.

He squatted by the fire with his arms folded and surveyed the four prisoners. Frank and Joe had been dragged back to the cave with the others and were now bound and helpless, while the gangsters confronted them.

"Who are these two?" asked the man called Pete, indicating the Hardy boys.

Red shook his head.

"We've seen 'em before. They were in the boat the day we were looking these two birds over," he remarked, gesturing toward Chet and Biff.

"What's your names?" demanded Pete gruffly.

The Hardy boys glanced at one another. Their captors were not yet aware of their identity and they did not know whether to admit it or not. Frank resolved on silence as the best course.

"Find out!" he retorted.

An ugly look crept into Red's face.

"Is that so?" he snarled. "Won't talk, eh? I'll soon make you talk."

He leaned forward and wrenched open Frank's coat. Frank's wrists were handcuffed and he was helpless to resist. Red pulled him roughly to one side and groped in the inner pocket of the coat. There was a rustle of paper and he withdrew two or three letters. Frank bit his lip in exasperation. He had forgotten about the letters and he knew that any hope of concealing his identity was now lost.

The red-headed man brought the letters over to the fire and squinted at the addresses. His eyes opened wide; his jaw dropped.

"Frank Hardy!" he gasped.

"What?" demanded one of the other men.

"All these letters are addressed to Frank Hardy!" declared the astonished gangster. "What d'you know about that!"

With a sudden movement, Pete grasped Joe by the collar and held him while he turned his pockets inside out. Finally, with an air of triumph, he produced Joe's membership card in a Bayport athletic association, on which his name was written in full.

"Joe Hardy!" he read. "Why, these are the real Hardy boys!"

The gangsters looked at one another with crestfallen expressions, but their momentary astonishment at realization of their mistake was quickly changed to rejoicing.

"I told you we weren't the Hardys," put in Chet. "I told you all along that you were making a mistake."

"Shut up!" ordered Red. "Yes, men, we made a mistake, all right. We didn't have the Hardy boys after all. But now we have got 'em! I'll say this is a piece of luck! We've got the whole caboodle now."

Meanwhile one of the men had been going more thoroughly through the boys' pockets. Now he grunted.

"Armed! Would you believe it? Brats like these!"

"Take the guns away," came the order from Red.

"What'll we do with the others?" demanded one of the gangsters.

"With the two we caught in the first place? We'll hang right onto 'em. We'll hold the Hardy boys for ransom the way we intended to, and we'll make some money out of the other two as well. You two boys," he said, turning to Chet and Biff, "have your people got money?"

"Find out!" snapped Chet, following Frank's example.

"We'll find out, all right!" rasped Pete. "We'll find out. And if they haven't got money it'll be all the worse for the pack of you!" He chuckled suddenly. "We'll make a real haul out of this, men! Four ransoms!"

"Yes, and now that we have the real Hardy boys we'll give Fenton Hardy a few anxious minutes," laughed another of the men, from a dark corner of the cave.

"Where is our father?" asked Frank.

Red scratched his chin meditatively.

"You're gettin' curious, hey? Want to know where your father is? I'll tell you. He's in a safe place where he can't get out of. Our men out in the West got him."

"What are they going to do with him?"

"Ah!" said Red, with an air of mystery. "What are they goin' to do with him? That's the question. One thing is certain—they're goin' to let him live until we collect ransom for you two."

"And after that?"

"After that? Well, it's up to the boss. But I'm thinkin' he'll never let Fenton Hardy loose again. He's too dangerous. Maybe, now, my young friends—"

"Don't talk too much, Red," warned Pete, stirring the fire. "Put these kids all in the inner cave and let's go to sleep again."

"I guess you're right, Pete," agreed the

red-headed man. "It don't pay to let 'em know too much."

With that, the Hardy boys and their two chums were bundled into the other cave, where a long chain was passed beneath the links of their handcuffs and passed through a staple embedded in the rock. The chain was fastened with a heavy padlock. Frank's heart sank as he heard the padlock snapped. There seemed to be no hope of escape now. They were securely chained together in the darkness of the inner cave.

Their captors left them.

"I guess you'll be safe enough in there until morning," grunted Pete as he departed, last of all. The gangsters returned to their fire and, after a brief discussion in low tones, they wrapped themselves up in their blankets once more.

The boys talked in whispers. Chet and Biff were anxious to know how the Hardy boys had followed them to the island and, in a few words, Frank told them of the alarm their disappearance had occasioned and of how they had decided to take a chance on searching Blacksnake Island.

"If only we could have got away!" muttered Joe. "We'd have been out toward the mainland in the boat by now!"

"If even one of us could have got away he

could have gone for help,'' Frank whispered.
''Oh, well—here we are, and we have to make
the best of it!''

''I'm worried about what they said about
dad.''

''So am I. We've simply *got* to get out of
here. If we can get word to the Chicago police
they may be able to find him before it's too
late!''

The boys were silent. The news that Fenton Hardy had been captured and that he was
in the hands of a merciless gang cast a cloud
of gloom over them all. They realized only
too well their own helplessness in the situation.

''I'm going to try to smash the lock on this
pair of handcuffs,'' Joe whispered finally. ''It
seemed rusty to me, when they put them on.''

''We tried that with ours,'' whispered Chet.
''It wasn't any use.''

''I may have better luck.''

''Wait until you're sure the gang are
asleep,'' whispered Biff. ''They might hear
you.''

The boys lapsed into silence. The darkness
of the cave was impenetrable. Near the entrance they could see a faint glow of pink from
the embers of the fire in the outer cavern, but
that was all. They could not even see one another.

The fact that tney were chained together

made it impossible for them to rest comfortably. The gangsters had not even provided them with a blanket.

"We've been chained in here every night since they caught us," Chet whispered. "We've had to sleep on the bare rock."

Finally the silence was broken by the sound of steel against rock. Joe was trying to break the lock of his handcuffs. The effort was difficult, because his hands were cuffed behind him. But, as he had said, the handcuffs were rusty and of an antiquated type. Against the hard rock he could feel them gradually giving way.

For more than ten minutes he battered the lock, the steel digging into his wrists. He worked as quietly as possible, with long intervals between each attempt. For a while he was afraid the effort would be fruitless, as even the rusty steel seemed obdurate. Then, suddenly, he felt the lock give way. He eased his hands out of the cuffs with a sigh of relief.

"I'm free," he whispered to the others.

There were suppressed exclamations of delight.

"How are you going to get us out?" whispered Frank.

"I'll try to find the keys."

A low murmur from the other cave arrested his attention. Swiftly he leaned back against

the wall. One of the gangsters was awake.
The boys listened. They heard a movement
in the outer cave, a jangling of keys, and then
a heavy footstep.

Joe thrust his arms behind his back and
feigned slumber. He could hear some one entering their cave.

Suddenly a bright light flashed in his face.
The man on guard had come to inspect the
captives and he brought with him a flashlight.
Joe kept his eyes closed and breathed heavily.
He hoped desperately that the man would not
inspect their handcuffs.

The fellow appeared satisfied and in a few
moments went away. Through narrowed eye-
lids Joe could see his dark form as he reached
the passage between the two caves. He saw
the round white circle of light shine for a moment on a small rock shelf in the passageway
and he saw the guard reach up and toss a
bundle of keys on the shelf. Then the man
went on his way, switching out the light.

Joe's heart beat faster.

This was luck for which he had not dared
hope. He now knew where the keys were kept.
Could he but reach them without arousing the
guard their chances of escape were multiplied
tenfold.

He waited until it seemed that hours had
passed. None of the boys dared so much as

whisper. The silence was profound. From the outer cave they could hear snores, but whether the guard was asleep or not they could not tell.

Joe realized that they would have to make their attempt before dawn, but he also knew that he could afford to wait, because the hours just before the break of day are the hours in which the average person sleeps most soundly, and there was every chance that the guard might be asleep by then as well.

At last he decided that it was time to act.

He got up quietly and began to make his way across the cave. Inch by inch he crawled across the rocky floor. He scarcely dared breathe for fear of disturbing one of their captors.

He was at the passage at last. The fire in the outer cave had died down. There was scarcely a vestige of light. This gave him hope, for it seemed to indicate that the guard had fallen asleep, otherwise he would have replenished the fire to protect himself against the night chill.

Joe groped for the little rock shelf. At first it eluded him, but at last his hand closed upon the keys. Carefully, he raised them, his hand clutching them tightly to prevent a betraying jangle of sound.

He turned slowly to make his way back to

the others. In silence he reached them and began to grope for the chain that bound them together. He found the chain at last, then the padlock, and felt in the darkness for the key to fit it.

The key at last! It was larger than the others, which he judged were the handcuff keys. The padlock snapped and he unhooked the chain.

"That's that," he whispered, quietly. "Now for the handcuffs."

One by one the other boys presented their shackled wrists to him in the darkness and he groped for the key that would set them free. In a tense silence he fumbled with the locks and the handcuffs but, one by one, the handcuffs opened, one by one the boys moved quietly aside, rubbing their chafed wrists.

At last the task was finished. They were free again.

But there still remained the outer cave!

CHAPTER XIX

Separated

Frank Hardy led the way.

He paused in the passage for a few seconds, surveying the scene in the outer cave.

All the men were asleep. They were rolled up in their blankets and lay sprawled in the shadows. There was merely a faint crimson glow from the embers of the fire.

He did not go on all fours; he just crouched low as he moved across the cave among the sleepers. Quick, sure footsteps, as silent as those of a cat, brought him to the outer entrance.

So much depended on their escape that the lads were uncannily silent. They seemed like mere shadows as they progressed, one by one, to the mouth of the cave. There was not a sound. The snores of the sleeping gangsters were unbroken.

Frank waited at the entrance. Chet joined him in a few moments. Then came Biff, and finally Joe. Safely out of the cave, the boys halted for a second on the rocks.

"I'll take the lead," whispered Frank. "Join hands and follow me."

It was pitch dark and the rocky path to the outskirts of the wood, he knew, would be treacherous. He reached back and grasped Chet's hand. Then he moved forward, carefully testing every step. On him depended the success of their flight to the wood. One stumble, one dislodged rock, might ruin everything.

Step by step, he moved cautiously forward. He had a good idea of where the woods trail opened, and he made toward it. Once they reached the trail he felt sure they would be safe.

Frank had an idea. He stopped and turned to the others.

"If anything happens," he said, in a low voice, "don't stick together. Scatter and try to make for the boat. Even if only one of us makes it he'll be able to get to the mainland."

The others whispered assent. He turned and proceeded across the rocks.

This safeguard, he felt, was wise. In case the gangsters discovered their escape they would prevent a repetition of the previous occurrence. In the darkness it was entirely probable that at least one, if not more, would be able to evade recapture.

But as he went on, his hopes rose. There was still not a sound from the cave in the rock. The darkness was in heavy silence.

He could faintly discern the black mass of trees and bushes before him. If they could only reach the trail!

But when he eventually came to the undergrowth he found that he had somehow missed the path. The trees were densely massed before him. They would be certain to raise a commotion if they attempted to enter the thicket at that point, he knew. They would be certain of becoming lost as well. They must find the trail.

Every moment was precious. Frank moved to the left but the bushes were still dense in front of him.

Joe moved up beside him.

"I think the trail is farther over," he said quietly.

Frank turned in the direction indicated.

They found the trail at last. Joe and Frank were ahead. Chet and Biff followed. Here they were unable to avoid making some sound. Twigs and branches crackled underfoot. This was unavoidable, but every noise seemed deafening.

Suddenly, from behind them, arose a terrific uproar.

Shouts, yells, the crash of a revolver, heavy

footfalls, rent the silence into shreds. The sounds came from the cave.

"They're gone!" roared a voice. "Wake up! They're gone!"

The boys remained stock-still for a moment in the gloom of the trail.

"They'll be after us," said Frank quickly. "Take it easy. Make for the cove. I'll take the lead. Make as little noise as you can."

He started off at a trot, and the others followed. Behind them the uproar increased in volume. They could hear the gangsters shouting to one another; they could hear rocks clattering as their pursuers came running down from the cave.

Their erstwhile captors were rushing directly for the trail. They assumed that the boys would attempt to regain their boat as quickly as possible.

A voice was shouting:

"Head them off at the shore! Don't let them get to their boat!"

The boys increased their speed. There was no attempt at concealment now. They could hear the branches crashing behind them as the gangsters hurried through the thicket.

In the pitch blackness of the grove they stumbled and fell, tripped and reeled as they rushed along.

Chet and Biff, being unused to the trail, were

obliged to travel at a slower pace, and in this way they dropped behind. The Hardy boys did not notice. There was such a confusion of sound in the grove, what with the noise of their own flight and the uproar of the pursuit, that they did not know that their chums were straggling.

At a fork in the trail, Frank and Joe headed to the left, the path leading downhill at this point, and toward the cove. They could hear the boom of the surf not far away and they knew that they were nearing their goal.

When Chet and Biff hastened up they failed to notice, in the inky blackness, that the trail branched two ways. Chet was in the lead and his footsteps brought him to the right. He could not hear the footsteps of the Hardy boys ahead but he judged that they were so far in advance that he could not hear them.

Their pursuers had become scattered. Some were pursuing them down the trail. Others were skirting the grove, intending to watch the shore. In the distance they could see occasional flashes of light. Once or twice there was a revolver shot.

"It won't go so well with us if they see us this time," called Frank back to his brother.

"If we can only beat them to the boat we'll be all right," panted Joe.

They emerged from the grove. They could see the white line of the surf ahead and the gray shapes of the rocks along the shore. The cove lay below.

The Hardy boys raced down the rocky slope. Only then did they become aware of the fact that their chums were not following.

Frank stopped and turned.

"Where are Chet and Biff?" he asked, startled.

"I thought they were right behind," replied Joe blankly.

They listened. There were no sounds of running footsteps down the trail. Back in the grove they could hear a frenzied crackling of branches, but whether it was caused by their comrades or by their pursuers they could not tell.

"They must have taken the wrong turning in the dark," declared Frank, as the solution dawned on him. "Quick—we'll get to the boat first! If we can find them we'll bring them with us. If we can't we'll have to make for the mainland alone."

A flash of scarlet light showed against the blackness of the bush as a revolver crashed out, and a scattering of rock close by told them that the bullet had been meant for them. The gangsters were near at hand.

Without another word the Hardy boys turned

and dashed down the rocky trail leading to the cove. The path was precipitous and rocky. Joe stumbled once and fell headlong, but he was up again in an instant, spurred on by the fear that they would be recaptured. Frank reached the shore first. The motorboat was just where they had left it, but it was drawn up on the sands.

Joe raced up and the boys placed themselves, one on either side of the bow.

"All right!" gritted Frank. "Ready!"

They shoved desperately at the motorboat, and it began to move slowly out into the water of the cove.

The gangsters were drawing closer. The boys heard heavy footfalls on the rocks at the outskirts of the grove.

Bang! Bang!

The revolver crashed out again. Bullets splashed into the water. Desperately, the Hardy boys struggled with their boat.

At last the keel left the sand, and the boat slid out swiftly into the cove waters. Frank and Joe splashed out into the waves and began to scramble over the side.

Frank had a glimpse of a dark figure racing down the rocky slope toward them. He leaped to the engine.

"Here they are!" roared a voice.

More footsteps came running along the shore.

The gangsters were converging toward the cove. Frank worked hastily over the engine. There was a splutter and a roar as the motor responded. The boat began to back slowly out of the cove.

"Keep down," he cautioned his brother.

Joe ducked, and not a moment too soon, for a fusillade of shots suddenly crashed out from the shore. Bullets whistled overhead. Wood splintered as one of them struck the side of the boat. Frank heard a heavy splashing in the water and judged that one of the gangsters was wading out in pursuit.

The boat moved slowly out to the entrance of the cove. In the darkness it was a ticklish performance. Frank doubted if he could make it. At any time it demanded careful steersmanship, and now there was no time for caution. The cove entrance was merely a faint gray blur against the darkness of the rocks on either side. He guided the *Sleuth* toward it.

Shots crashed and echoed from the shore. A dark form suddenly rose up beside the boat, with revolver upraised, but Joe launched himself on the man with surprising suddenness. His fist shot out and crashed into the gangster's face. With a muffled cry, the fellow stumbled back and lost his balance, going beneath the waves. He rose again in a moment, waist-deep in water, spluttering and choking, but by that time the *Sleuth* was several yards away and the water was too deep to permit the fellow to wade out any farther. His revolver was useless, and he began to make his way back to shore, growling to himself.

The motorboat reached the cove entrance. The rocks loomed high on either side.

Frank held his breath. At any moment he expected to hear the dread sound of the scraping rocks, but the *Sleuth* glided through the narrow channel without mishap, then shot out to the open sea. He spun the wheel about, brought the boat forward, and a moment later the engine was roaring its staccato defiance to the gangsters in the cove.

Frank looked back. He could see flashlights bobbing up and down on the beach.

"They're going for their own boats!" he exclaimed.

Then, with a grim smile, he bent forward over the wheel. Instead of heading the motorboat out to the open sea, he directed it along the shore, toward the distant cove where the gangsters had hidden their own craft.

CHAPTER XX

SEIZING THE BOATS

"WHAT are you going to do, Frank?" shouted Joe Hardy.

"They're going after their boats. We know the cove they're in, and if we can get there first I'll tow them out to sea. Then they can't follow us!"

Thus Frank briefly outlined his daring scheme to his brother. He knew that the gangsters would not expect any such intention and he knew as well that only by some action of this kind could he avoid danger of capture. If the gangsters followed in their own boats there was every chance that they might overtake or outmaneuver the *Sleuth*. Even if they did not, as long as they retained possession of their own motorboats they could make good their escape. But once marooned on the island, they would be at the mercy of the Hardy boys.

"We'll have to hurry!" said Joe anxiously.

He watched the progress of the flashlights on the shore. The *Sleuth* was well ahead, but the seizure of the boats would take some time. The gangsters were making their way slowly over the rocks on their way to the cove.

Frank increased the speed of the boat. It leaped through the waves, the motor roaring. The flashlights on the shore were left far behind.

"We'll make it!" he shouted gleefully to Joe, the spray dashing against his face. He could distinguish the jutting headland that told him the location of the coves.

The men on the shore finally seemed to realize his intention. The boys could now hear frantic shouts as the men called to one another and made desperate efforts to reach the boats. But the *Sleuth* had outstripped them and they were left stumbling among the rocks along the beach.

The motorboat swept around the headland and into the cove. Frank had switched on the searchlight above the bow, and in its glare he could see the two motorboats belonging to the gang.

It was the work of but a minute to bring the *Sleuth* alongside, for the craft were riding at anchor. Joe seized a length of rope from the stern, then stood in readiness while his brother brought the *Sleuth* close to the side of the first craft. He leaped lightly into the other motorboat, lashed one end of the rope to the bow, then returned to the *Sleuth* again, tying the loose end of the rope securely, so that the motorboat could be towed.

Swiftly, Frank brought his boat around to the bow of the remaining craft, where the process was repeated. Joe snubbed one end of a length of stout rope to the bow, the other to the stern of the next boat. The two craft were now ready to be towed away by the *Sleuth*.

There was a sharp clattering of rock from among the bluffs near the cove. Then a shout:

"Red! They're stealing the boats!"

"Head 'em off!" roared another voice frantically from behind. "Don't let them get away!"

But already the engine of the *Sleuth* was roaring its message of triumph to the pursuers. Slowly, the motorboat began to make its way out of the cove.

And slowly, the ropes tightened. The two motorboats began moving behind. Joe had raised the anchor in each case and the craft were free to follow the lead boat.

There was a yell of dismay from the shore.

"They're starting out! They've got the boats!"

This was followed by a fusillade of shots. The man on the beach opened fire, and his companion farther back among the rocks did likewise. Bullets whistled past the *Sleuth*. But, in the darkness, the men on shore could take but indifferent aim. Frank had switched out the headlight and the gangsters could see only a ghostly gray shadow on the water.

The *Sleuth* picked up speed and the two motorboats behind began to rock and sway as they surged forward. Frank knew that he could not go too fast, otherwise the boats that he was towing would run foul of one another or of his own craft and cause disaster. He contented himself by moving ahead at a moderate rate of speed, knowing well that once he cleared the cove he could afford to snap his fingers at the gangsters marooned on the island.

Shouts interspersed with revolver shots told him of their pursuers' wrath. The flashlights danced like fireflies. The full extent of the trick that had been played upon them was just beginning to dawn on the men marooned on the shore.

The headland loomed to the side, then slipped slowly by. The motorboat was throbbing its way out to open water.

"We've beaten 'em," declared Frank exultantly.

"I'll say we have! They'll never get off that island unless they swim."

"From the fuss they're making, they seem to know it, too."

"Where to now?"

"The mainland. If we can get to Rock Harbor we'll get help."

"How about Chet and Biff?" asked Joe soberly.

"We can't afford to take a chance on bringing them off the island just now. I hate to desert them, but we can't do anything else. If we went back for them we'd likely undo everything we've done so far. But I think they'll be safe enough. They'll hide in the bushes. Those fellows have been so busy chasing us that they haven't had any time to worry about them."

"Perhaps they think we all got away."

"If they do they won't be hunting around for Chet and Biff. In any case, we had the agreement that even if only one of us got away he would come back with help for the rest. They'll know we'll be back."

"So will the gangsters. I'll bet they're worrying about how they can clear away from this island before we get back."

Frank headed the boat for the mainland. It was his intention, as he had said, to make his way to Rock Harbor, where they could secure help—officers and men to come back with them to Blacksnake Island to aid in the rescue of their chums and in the capture of the gangsters.

There was the chance, of course, that the

latter might have a canoe or a skiff hidden somewhere on the island, but he did not think they would trust themselves to the open water of the channel in any such frail craft. He felt convinced that by seizing the two motorboats they had effectually marooned their enemies.

They passed the last jutting point of the sinister island and the bow of the *Sleuth* was headed toward the coast.

"Perhaps we won't have to go all the way to Rock Harbor," suggested Joe. "If we could meet a ship we might get help."

"It seems to me I see a light now. Running low on the water. Do you see it?"

Joe peered into the darkness.

"I believe you're right," he said finally. "It seems to be coming this way, too."

"Perhaps some more of the gang."

"I hadn't thought of that. Better not go too close."

Frank eyed the approaching light warily. It was just a faint gleam in the darkness and he judged it was from a motorboat which was most certainly bound toward Blacksnake Island. Eventually he could hear the steady throb of the engine.

After a moment or so he started up excitedly.

"Joe! I'd know that engine anywhere."

"So would I! It's—"

"The *Napoli!*"

He spun the wheel about so that the *Sleuth* would cut across the bows of the approaching craft. Steadily, through the darkness, came the throbbing of the engine, and as the boat came closer the Hardy boys became more and more convinced that it was Tony Prito's craft.

"I've been wondering what became of him," Frank declared. "When he didn't show up earlier I began to think he must have had to call off the trip."

"It may not be him after all, but I'm sure it's his boat. If it isn't I'll never believe my ears again."

The two boats approached one another. Frank shut down the engine of the *Sleuth*, rose from his seat, and shouted:

"*Napoli*, ahoy!"

Almost immediately the roar of the other engine died to a murmur and a well-known voice replied:

"This is the *Napoli*. Who are you?"

It was the voice of Tony Prito. Joe gave a yell of delight.

"It's us!" shouted Frank. "The Hardy boys!"

They could hear sounds of excited talking in the other boat, and a suppressed cheer.

"Coming over!" Tony called out, and in a few minutes the two boats had drawn up alongside. In the glare of the headlight Frank and Joe could see Tony Prito, Jerry Gilroy and Phil Cohen.

Their greetings were cut short when the boys saw the two trailing boats and Frank tersely explained the situation.

"You couldn't have come at a better time. We found Chet and Biff on the island. They're still there. We tried to escape, but got separated and only Joe and I got away. Chet and Biff are in hiding somewhere and we stole the other motorboats."

"Whose motorboats?" asked Jerry.

"Chet and Biff were captured by a gang of crooks who mistook them for us. These fellows had a cave on the island and two motorboats of their own. When we made our get-away we towed their boats away with us so the men are all marooned there."

A chorus of excited questions broke forth as the newcomers demanded further details, but Frank went on:

"We're going to the mainland for help. What we want you to do is take charge of these two motorboats and keep cruising around the island to see that the gang doesn't get away."

"Good!" approved Phil. "And if we can pick up Chet and Biff we'll do it."

"If you can, without letting the gang get hold of those boats again."

"Fine!" Tony declared. "We'll take the boats. Throw over that rope."

He caught the rope deftly, and the captured motorboats were soon being towed by the *Napoli,* leaving the Hardy boys' craft free for its flight to the mainland.

"We'll be back as soon as we can," called out Frank.

"We'll be watching for you."

"Good. No use wasting any more time. Good luck!"

"Good luck!" shouted the others.

Frank bent over the wheel again. The engine of the *Sleuth* roared as the speedy craft turned toward the mainland. The *Napoli,* in its turn, began to forge ahead toward Blacksnake Island, its speed somewhat lessened now by the drag of the captured boats. Tony, Jerry and Phil were agog with excitement over this strange encounter in the darkness and the sensational news the Hardy boys had given them.

So the two motorboats went their separate ways in the darkness of the night—one to the mainland, the other toward the sinister island where Chet Morton and Biff Hooper were marooned with the gangsters.

CHAPTER XXI

In the meantime, what of Chet Morton and Biff Hooper?

When they took the wrong turn in the trail it was some time before they realized that the Hardy boys were not running along before them. They were blundering along through the undergrowth, in complete darkness, trusting to their chums to guide them through, when finally Chet stopped, panting.

"Frank and Joe must be running like deer," he muttered. "I can't hear them at all."

"We were all mighty close together a little while ago," returned Biff.

"I know. And they seem to have disappeared all of a sudden." The thought struck Chet that they might be on the wrong trail. "Do you think we could have taken a wrong turn?"

Biff listened. "There's no one ahead of us, that's sure," he said at last. "We must have got separated."

186

As this conviction forced itself upon them, the two lads were overwhelmed with disappointment. They knew that the Hardy boys would have little enough time to gain the boat and escape without waiting for them, and at the thought that they might be again left on the island at the mercy of their captors they were profoundly discouraged.

"We're up against it again, I guess," declared Chet. "Well, I think we'd better follow this trail anyway, wherever it leads to. Remember what Frank said—that if even one of us reached the boat safely he could get to the mainland and bring back help for the rest."

"Yes, that's right. It isn't as bad as it might be."

"I only hope the gang don't capture them before they make the boat safely. Listen!"

They stopped in their tracks and listened as the night wind bore to their ears the sound of gunfire from the beach. It was far over to one side of them. They could hear distant shouts, then the spasmodic firing of revolvers followed again.

"They must be having a sweet time. I guess the gang are trying to keep them from getting the boat," said Chet.

Then they heard the muffled roar of the motorboat in the cove.

"They're getting away!" declared Biff, in

excitement. "You can hear the boat backing out."

More revolver shots—more shouts—the roar of the *Sleuth's* engine continued.

"As long as they get away safely I'm not worrying much," Chet said. "Just the same, I'd rather be with them. But they'll bring back help."

"In the meantime, the best thing we can do is to hide."

"The gang will be scouring the island for us now that they know we didn't get away with the others. And they won't be any too gentle with us either, if they get us."

Chet and Biff decided that it would be best to get as near the shore as possible before concealing themselves, so as to be ready for a rush to safety should the Hardy boys return with the promised assistance. By the sound of the motorboat and the shooting, they judged that the narrow trail led toward the shore, so they followed it as well as they could in the darkness. The wet branches slashed their faces and they stumbled over roots and slipped in the wet, deep grass, but gradually the sound of the breaking surf drew closer and they knew they were coming nearer to the beach.

The path suddenly dipped and they descended a slope, finally emerging from the trees to find themselves on a rocky hillside overlooking the

gray shore. They could see the white foam of
the breaking rollers, and the gray rocks below
but there was no sign of motorboat or of any
human being.

"We may as well stay right on this hillside,
behind the rocks," Chet suggested. "If we go
roaming about the shore we're likely to run
into Red and his gang."

"Perhaps they've taken their own boats and
gone after the Hardy boys."

"They may have. But we can't take a chance
on it. If any of them are prowling around it
would be just our luck to meet them."

The chums made themselves as comfortable
as possible in the shelter of a huge rock, from
which they had a good view of the shore and
the sea beyond. It was still dark and they had
little hope of rescue before morning.

"It'll take them quite a while to get to the
mainland and rouse any one to come out here
to help us," remarked Chet. "The big thing
is for us to keep hidden until daylight and then
lay low until we see a chance of rescue."

"You can trust me to lay low. I've no
hankering to be dragged back to that cave
again."

"Me neither."

The boys lapsed into silence. They realized
that conversation was dangerous. At any
moment some member of the gang might be

venturing near and might hear their voices.

From a distant side of the island they suddenly heard more shots. They broke out in a perfect fusillade of gunfire, and the rocks flung back the echoes, mingled with yells of rage. At the same time, they again heard the sound of the *Sleuth's* engine, slower this time, as though the craft were but crawling along.

"I can't understand this," said Chet. "We heard them leave the cove a little while ago. Now they're away down the shore and going slow."

"Perhaps they're having engine trouble," said Biff mournfully.

"I can't figure it out at all. It's tough to be sitting here in the dark, not knowing whether they've got away or not."

"I don't dare let myself think they haven't got away," declared Biff, with determination.

An hour passed. The sounds of the motor-boat had long since died away. Once in a while the chums heard voices back in the grove and they knew that at least some of the gangsters had been left on the island. Whether the others had left in pursuit of the Hardy boys, they could not tell. Had they known of the Hardys' *coup* in taking the gangsters' two boats they would have felt more relieved in mind. The chill of approaching morning had settled over the island, and they huddled together in the shelter of the rock, seeking warmth.

Suddenly, from the sea, they heard the steady chug-chug of a motorboat that seemed to be progressing slowly along in close proximity to the shore. They looked out and they could see a headlight slowly moving through the darkness.

"It's a motorboat, but it's traveling very slowly," said Chet.

"Let's take a chance and hail them."

"It might be some of the gang."

"That's right. But we can go down closer to the shore and see. It may be Frank and Joe looking for us."

The two lads left the shelter of the rocks and began moving cautiously toward the beach. They realized that there was every chance that the mysterious craft might be one of the gangsters' boats and that they would be risking recapture by making their presence known. But, on the other hand, it might be the Hardy boys returning in an effort to pick them up.

They had gone no more than a few yards when a loud voice only a short distance away made them jump with surprise:

"Is that one of our boats, Pete?"

"No. I don't know it at all. There's something funny about this."

A rock clattered down the slope. Chet looked

back. Two dark figures appeared in sight at the top of the declivity.

The two parties saw one another at the same time.

"Here they are!" roared one of the men, and he plunged down the slope straight at the astonished boys.

The other man came running after him. The first impulse of the two chums was to run, but they saw that flight would be useless. They were midway on the hillside leading to the beach and the path was treacherous with rocks and loose gravel. They would be overtaken in a moment.

"Fight 'em!" said Chet, gritting his teeth.

The boys stood their ground. The two gangsters, one of whom they recognized as Pete, came floundering down the slope. They had started out in such a rush that now they were not well able to stop, and as the pair came at them the two chums braced themselves for the shock.

Biff met the first man squarely. His passion for boxing now stood him in good stead. He judged his distance perfectly. As the fellow came at him, arms swinging, he drove a straight left to the fellow's midriff.

The gangster gasped and doubled up with pain. He wavered for a moment, then Biff swung. His right fist crashed against the man's jaw, and the gangster toppled over on his face. He rolled over in the gravel a few times, then came to a stop, sprawled senseless on the hillside.

As for Chet, he made use of strategy. When the second man rushed at him he sidestepped neatly.

His right foot went out. The gangster tripped over it and, so great had been the force of his rush and so sudden was his downfall, that he went ploughing forward on his face for several yards until he came to a ledge of rock. He made frantic efforts to save himself as he felt that he was going over the side, but his descent could not be checked. Chet had a glimpse of desperately waving arms and kicking legs; then his adversary disappeared with a crash. The ledge was only a few feet from the beach, but it was certain that the fall would knock the breath out of the gangster's body for several minutes at least.

Without another word the boys scrambled back up the hillside. They knew that the gangsters would recover quickly and that the alarm would soon be sounded. They must hide, and that quickly.

They gained the shelter of the bushes just as the gangster who had gone tumbling over the ledge began to find his breath again and shout for help. Desperately, the boys scrambled through the undergrowth, seeking no path, seeking only a hiding place.

At length, when they were in a dense thicket where the branches were so closely entwined that further progress seemed impossible, they halted.

"This is as far as we can go," panted Chet. "They'll be searching for us now, but they'll never find us in here."

"That was a narrow escape!"

"It sure was. But we gave them something to remember us by."

Biff Hooper doubled up his fist with satisfaction.

"I knocked my man colder than a sardine," he declared.

It was nearing dawn. The first faint streaks of light were appearing in the eastern sky.

"I wonder where that boat went," said Chet suddenly. "Perhaps it's still near the island."

"It wasn't one of the boats belonging to the gang, anyway, by the way those two fellows were talking. If we could get a hiding place a little nearer the shore we might be able to see it."

"Yes—let's get out of this thicket."

Quietly, the boys began to withdraw from the deep thicket in which they had become entangled. But the branches cracked underfoot and seemed to have the brittleness of matchwood. The chums were afraid they would be heard.

"Better stay where we are," muttered Chet.

They remained motionless for some time, and the swift dawn soon began to paint the sky. The darkness diminished and the boys could now see one another plainly, and could see the extent of the deep thicket in which they had become enmeshed.

"Now let's try to get out," said Chet.

Again they attempted to make their way out of the thicket, and this time, because they could see what they were doing, their efforts met with more success. But they could not avoid making considerable noise, and the crackling of branches seemed like the reports of rifles.

Then, to their horror, they heard a voice:

"I heard a noise in the bushes over there almost an hour ago, and now I hear it again."

"We'll go over and see," replied another voice.

The boys looked at one another, then froze into silence. They could hear heavy footfalls near by. Branches crackled.

"They're hiding around on this side of the island somewhere," said the first voice. "If I ever lay my hands on 'em—"

Chet put his finger to his lips as a warning to silence, but there was no need. Biff was scarcely daring to breathe.

Just at that moment a sound broke forth that sent a thrill of fear through them both.

It was a sibilant, terrifying hiss, right at their feet.

Chet looked down and gave a low cry. A huge blacksnake was coiled in the grass, in readiness to strike.

CHAPTER XXII

THE CHASE

CHET MORTON leaped back with such violence that he collided with his chum. He had seen the serpent in the nick of time, and his backward leap had been so instinctive and so involuntary that he somehow evaded the swift, whiplike thrust of the evil head that plunged at him.

The snake missed, although its body writhed against Chet's boot for a second and the fangs stabbed against the heavy leather. The boot saved the boy. Had the snake struck against his leg he would have been bitten.

The chums plunged blindly through the thicket.

There was no thought of caution now. They were filled with unreasoning terror of the blacksnake, the instinctive revulsion that fills most people at the sight of such a reptile, and they went crashing through the bushes. The noise of their flight did not escape the two rascals who had been searching for them.

"I see them!" shouted one of the men. He came plunging through the deep grass at the outskirts of the thicket to intercept the boys.

Chet saw him in time and veered to one side. He just managed to evade the outflung arm, then went running desperately to the top of the hillside overlooking the sea. Biff came thundering behind, outdistanced the second gangster, dodged the other man, and raced after Chet.

They went slipping and sliding down the slope. Chet had no clear idea of where they were bound, but he was determined to keep running either until he was captured or overcome with exhaustion.

But when he came over the brow of the hill and began the steep descent, he saw something in the sea below that made him give an exultant yell.

It was a motorboat, and one that he recognized immediately. The boat was none other than the *Napoli,* and in it were three figures. Even at that distance he knew them for Tony Prito, Phil Cohen and Jerry Gilroy. Behind the motorboat were two other craft, being towed.

He had not been seen as yet, for he saw that the *Napoli* was cruising leisurely around the island. He shouted hoarsely to attract attention.

He saw Tony look up, then speak excitedly to his comrades. They waved frantically in reply. Then the bow of the *Napoli* began to head in toward the shore.

Could they reach the boat in safety? Biff was thundering down the slope only a few feet behind Chet. Rocks and pebbles went bouncing and bounding along in front of them; sand and gravel flew from about their boots. And, coming in swift pursuit, were the two gangsters who had so nearly captured them in the thicket. These men were shouting hoarsely to them to stop.

But the two chums had no intention of stopping. They saw safety in sight. Could they reach the shore and gain the boat before the two gangsters overtook them?

Then, out from among the rocks along the beach emerged three figures. Chet's heart sank. They were the other gangsters and they were directly in the path. At the same time, he saw that Tony Prito was bringing the *Napoli* around, and away from the shore.

Spent and exhausted, he tried to dodge the three men ahead, but the effort was short-lived. One of the three leaped forward and grappled with him. They fell struggling into the sand. The other two leaped at Biff.

The boys fought bravely and desperately. Chet struck out and his fist crashed into the face of the man who had tackled him. The fellow sagged back for a second and Chet tried to free himself from the grasp around his waist, but as he did so one of the other two gangsters came rushing up and launched himself on him.

Biff battled with equal ferocity, but he was powerless against the three rascals. He kicked and struggled, but they had him down and they dragged him back behind the rocks, where the others soon brought Chet.

The red-headed man, with a bruise over one eye, produced a length of stout cord from his hip pocket.

"Tie 'em up!" he snapped. "We've got 'em this time for keeps."

Pete grabbed the cord, and in a few minutes Chet's wrists were bound tightly behind his back and his ankles were securely tied. Pete cut the cord and used the remainder for binding Biff. The two chums were helpless.

As for Tony Prito, in the *Napoli,* he had quickly seen that it would be impossible, even foolhardy, to attempt to rescue his two chums. In the first place, there were five boys against five men, the latter desperate and fully armed. The only result would be the capture of them all and the capture, as well, of the three motorboats by the gangsters.

"I hate to see them caught with us so close,

but what can we do?'' he said, turning to the others, as he slowly brought the *Napoli* around.

"If the men catch us and the motorboats, the boys will only be worse off than they were before.''

"I guess you're right,'' agreed Jerry Gilroy. "I sure thought for a minute that we were going to be able to save them. Between the crowd of us we could have held off those other two toughs long enough to get Chet and Biff on board, but when the others showed up I knew it was all off.''

"The fellows put up a good fight, anyway,'' declared Phil Cohen. "I hope those villains don't treat 'em too rough.''

"We'll get them free yet,'' asserted Tony. "I don't know how it's going to be done, but we'll get 'em free. We've still got all the motorboats and the gang can't leave the island, that's sure.''

When he had brought the *Napoli* out a safe distance from shore, Tony decided to drop anchor.

"We'll stick around,'' he decided. "They'll know that we aren't going to desert them anyway.''

So the *Napoli,* with the two captured motorboats drifting behind, remained at anchor, while the three chums scanned the rocky shore. Once in a while they saw one or another of the gangsters emerging from behind the boulders to gaze at them, then return.

"We've got them guessing," chuckled Tony. "They don't know what to make of us. They know we have their boats, but they don't know who we are or how we got 'em."

Two hours passed. The sun rose higher in the sky. Blacksnake Island, in all its sinister ugliness, simmered in the morning heat. There was no further sign of life from the shore. Although the boys in the motorboat did not know it, the boulders behind which Chet and Biff had been carried hid the trail up to the grove and thence to the cave in the rocks. The gangsters had decided to return to this cave and Chet and Biff, with their ankle bonds untied, had been roughly ordered to their feet and bade proceed with the gangsters up the hidden trial. They had not been seen from the boat because a heavy veil of overhanging branches from the trees masked the trail where it wound up the hillside.

Toward mid-morning Tony chanced to look up and gaze out toward the mainland. He leaped up with a frantic yell.

"Here they come!" he shrieked. "Here they are!"

The others rose and stared. Then, as the meaning of what they saw dawned on them, they cheered hoarsely, and danced with delight until the motorboat rocked and swayed beneath their feet.

Cleaving the waves, came a low, rakish craft, speeding along with white wings of foam at her prow. It rushed silently toward them with the grace of an arrow. It was a United States revenue cutter, and when the boys in the boat witnessed its approach they knew that the Hardy boys had been successful in obtaining the aid they had gone to seek.

The boys cheered and waved their arms, trying to signal to the cutter that they had located Chet and Biff. Finally, Tony started up the engine and brought the *Napoli* alongside. The cutter slowly came to a stop, there was a clank and a clatter as the anchor was sent over.

A husky revenue officer with a revolver strapped to his waist leaned over the side and hailed them.

"Did you find them?" he roared.

"They were caught again, right on this shore!" shouted Tony. "The gang are still here."

"Fine! We'll be right over. Tie your craft alongside and come along in our boat!"

The lads needed no second urging. A ladder was flung over the side and, after securely tying the *Napoli*, they clambered up on the deck of the cutter where they found the Hardy boys awaiting them.

In a few swift words Tony acquainted them with the circumstances surrounding the recapture of Chet and Biff. The revenue officer who had first hailed them nodded with satisfaction.

"As long as we know that those rascals haven't left the island, it's all right," he declared. "We'll have them in hand before long."

He turned and gave a curt order to one of his men and in a remarkably short space of time there were a dozen broad-shouldered chaps in readiness, with rifles and revolvers. Another order, and a boat was lowered over the side.

"Away we go!" announced the officer. "It won't be long now."

CHAPTER XXIII

Home Again

Tony Prito and his chums guided the landing party to the boulders behind which the gangsters and their captives had disappeared, but when Frank Hardy saw that the prey had flown he assumed the rôle of guide.

"They've gone up to the cave," he said. "I know the way."

With Joe, he went in advance of the party. Tony, Phil and Jerry came behind, with the officer and his men, their faces alight with anticipation of a battle, clambering up the hillside in their wake. The sturdy, tanned men were alert and ready for the approaching fight.

Through the grove, down the leafy trail, the Hardy boys led them, and at last they came within sight of the clearing. The great rock and the dark entrance of the cave were in sight. There was no sign of any human being.

"Deploy!" ordered the officer.

The men scattered. The Hardy boys and

their chums, being unarmed, were obliged to watch from the shelter of the grove, because they realized that there would probably be gunfire.

The men began to make their way across the open space, running from rock to rock, keeping well scattered, all eying the entrance to the cave.

Suddenly, a shot sounded from the cave entrance. Almost simultaneously one of the revenue men fired. The boys had seen no one in the cave but the keen eyes of the rifleman had, and when the body of a man slumped forward out of the cave, falling on the rocks, with a revolver clattering from his nerveless fingers, his judgment was verified.

And this, to the disappointment of the watchers, was the end of the fight. For the gangsters, like so many of their kind, were cowardly and they became unnerved at the fate of the first of their men who had shown fight.

Out of the cave entrance came a man bearing aloft a white handkerchief in token of surrender. He was followed by the others, with hands upraised, and behind them came Chet Morton and Biff Hooper, their wrists still bound, but their faces alight with joy, in contrast to the surly visages of the gangsters.

"Well, well!" declared the officer in charge, as he confronted the rascals, noting the frowning red-haired man. "If it isn't Red Hawkins and his gang! And you too, Pete! We've been looking for your hangout for the past three months—and for you as well. Put the cuffs on 'em, boys."

In a few moments the gang were securely handcuffed. The man who had been shot was attended to and it was found that he had been wounded, but after a brief examination and the rendering of first aid, the officer assured the victim that he would live to face trial with the rest for the abduction of Chet and Biff.

"And if that charge falls through—which it won't," he assured them all, "we have a list of other charges against you, as long as your arm."

But the Hardy boys and their chums were oblivious to this scene. They were too busy staging an impromptu reunion. Chet Morton and Biff Hooper, freed of their bonds, were busy shaking hands all round and trying to explain to their excited comrades some of the adventures they had gone through since leaving Bayport.

Then the Hardy boys were called on to explain how they had encountered the revenue cutter and how they had told their story and prevailed on the revenue men to come with them to Blacksnake Island to effect the rescue of their chums.

"But we can talk it over better on the way back," declared Frank.

"Coming back with us?" asked the officer. "We're taking these men to Rock Harbor, but you're welcome to come along."

"No thanks—we'll be going back in the motorboats."

"I see. Well, we'll take this gang back to the ship. Forward—march, you!" he shouted to the crestfallen gangsters.

So the party returned to the shore and Red Hawkins and his four men were herded into the boat. They had not said a word, but on their way back to the cutter Red turned to the Hardy boys and snarled:

"Well, you've got me, but our men in the West got your father. We've got that much satisfaction, anyway!"

With that he lapsed into silence, realizing that his words had the immediate effect of dampening the spirits of the Hardy boys and their chums.

Back at the revenue cutter, Frank and Joe said good-bye to the officer and his men, leaving Red and his gang in their charge. The motorboat had been towed behind the ship and they resumed their places in the *Sleuth* and cast away.

Tony Prito and the others took their places in the *Napoli* while Chet and Biff returned to the *Envoy*. One of the captured boats turned out to be none other than Biff's own craft, which the gangsters had been using while they were prisoners in the cave. Thus the journey home began.

Although there was rejoicing in the other boats and much good-natured badinage was passed about, the Hardy boys found it difficult to be cheerful. Red's words had brought back to them their fears concerning the safety of their father and they dreaded the news that might await them when they returned to Bayport.

"If there is no news from him, I think we should go to Chicago and search for him," said Frank gravely.

"I'm with you in that. But perhaps it won't be so bad. Red may have been only trying to frighten us."

"I hope so. If that was his object he sure succeeded."

"At any rate, we found the missing chums."

"Another feather in our cap, eh?" grinned Frank. "If dad does come back safely he won't have any reason to be ashamed of his sons."

"The Mortons and the Hoopers will be glad. The whole city will be in a fuss over what happened to Chet and Biff."

This proved to be the case. When the three motorboats returned to Barmet Bay and finally docked at Bayport they found a cheering throng awaiting them, for the news had been sent to the city by the revenue men from Rock Harbor, and the anxieties of the boys' families were set at rest. The Hoopers and Mortons, in particular, had been almost frantic with worry and Chet and Biff were given a welcome befitting heroes of an expedition given up for lost for many years.

Nor were the Hardy boys and their chums forgotten in the welcome. Chet and Biff gave full credit to the Hardys for the part they had played in the round-up of the gangsters. When Frank and Joe were finally able to break away from the crowd and make their way back home, the news of the exploit was beginning to spread rapidly through the city.

When they came within sight of the familiar house they broke into a run. They raced up the front steps. They flung open the front door and burst into the hallway, almost knocking over Aunt Gertrude, who was dusting.

"Lands sakes!" she exclaimed. "Can't you boys ever learn to come into a house properly? I never seen the like in all my born days! Go right back out that door and come in again like gentlemen!"

"Home again!" exclaimed Frank, with a grin. Then he turned anxiously to his aunt. "Any word yet from dad?"

"He's in the library!" sniffed Aunt Gertrude.

"In the library!" exclaimed the boys, in astonishment.

"Yes, in the library. And what of it? Where did you expect he'd be? Up in the attic?"

But the Hardy boys did not wait to reply. With a whoop of delight they rushed through the living room and into the library, where they found Fenton Hardy seated at the table. Their father got up quickly as they rushed at him, and in a moment all three were shaking hands and chattering in gladness and relief.

"We heard you'd been caught by the gang!" gasped Frank.

Fenton Hardy smiled. "It was the other way around," he corrected them. "The gang was caught by me."

"And we caught the rest of them!"

"Not Red Hawkins and his crew?"

The Hardy boys nodded. Their father gazed at them in incredulous astonishment for a moment. Then he slapped them heartily on the back and indicated the chairs near by.

"And I thought they'd clear out when they knew Baldy and the others were behind the bars! Why, this rounds up the entire pack! Tell me about it. But—first of all, have Chet and Biff been found?"

The boys nodded.

"We found them on Blacksnake Island. That's how we rounded up the gang. They captured Chet and Biff in mistake for us. They had 'em in a cave."

Then, in the seclusion of the study, the Hardy boys told of their search for the missing chums, of their deduction that the boys might have gone to Blacksnake Island, of their arrival on the island and the finding of the gangsters and their cave.

Fenton Hardy listened to the recital with sparkling eyes, for he realized that his sons had played a part that made him proud of them, and when the tale was finished his approval was evident by the manner in which he pounded the desk with his fist.

"Fine!" he declared. "It was real detective work in the first place and real grit and courage from then on. I'm very proud of my boys."

"But all the time," added Frank, "we were worried about you. The men said you had been captured in the West."

"It was a false report," said their father. "They thought they had captured me, but it wasn't for long. I played into their hands once, just to find out where they were all hiding. But I had another detective to shadow me and when I found out where the gang were gathered I gave the signal and we rounded them up.''

''And now I hope the whole kit and bilin' of you will stay at home for a while!'' declared a voice from the doorway. ''I declare I never did see such a family for the men-folks to go gallivantin' around the country and never stayin' at home. It's a wonder to me, Laura, that you put up with it.''

''Well,'' smilingly replied Mrs. Hardy, who had entered the room with Aunt Gertrude, ''with three first-rate detectives in the family, I'm afraid I can't expect anything else. And they always come home again.''

Aunt Gertrude sniffed.

''I'll guarantee that if I visit here much longer I'll see that those two boys haven't much chance for more detecting!'' she announced. ''I'll cure 'em, so I will. It's no business at all for boys.''

Mrs. Hardy smiled serenely.

Fenton Hardy winked gravely at his sons, so Aunt Gertrude's threat did not greatly disturb them.

There were to be more exciting adventures in store for the Hardy boys, and what some of these were will be related in the next volume of this series, entitled ''The Hardy Boys: Hunting for Hidden Gold,'' a strenuous story of the West.

"You're welcome to try, Aunt Gertrude," said Mr. Hardy; "but I'm afraid you'll never cure my sons of wanting to be detectives. I've set them the example, you see."

"More's the pity," sniffed Aunt Gertrude. "Why couldn't you have been a plumber? It's safer."

"But not as exciting," said Fenton Hardy, with a laugh.

THE END

This Isn't All!

Would you like to know what became of the good friends you have made in this book?

Would you like to read other stories continuing their adventures and experiences, or other books quite as entertaining by the same author?

On the *reverse side* of the wrapper which comes with this book, you will find a wonderful list of stories which you can buy at the same store where you got this book.

Don't throw away the Wrapper

Use it as a handy catalog of the books you want some day to have. But in case you do mislay it, write to the Publishers for a complete catalog.

GARRY GRAYSON FOOTBALL STORIES

By ELMER A. DAWSON

Individual Colored Wrappers and Illustrations by
WALTER S. ROGERS
Every Volume Complete in Itself

Football followers all over the country will hail with delight this new and thoroughly up-to-date line of gridiron tales.

Garry Grayson is a football fan, first, last, and all the time. But more than that, he is a wideawake American boy with a "gang" of chums almost as wideawake as himself.

How Garry organized the first football eleven his grammar school had, how he later played on the High School team, and what he did on the Prep School gridiron and elsewhere, is told in a manner to please all readers and especially those interested in watching a rapid forward pass, a plucky tackle, or a hot run for a touchdown.

Good, clean football at its best—and in addition, rattling stories of mystery and schoolboy rivalries.

GARRY GRAYSON'S HILL STREET ELEVEN;
    or, The Football Boys of Lenox.

GARRY GRAYSON AT LENOX HIGH; or, The
    Champions of the Football League.

GARRY GRAYSON'S FOOTBALL RIVALS; or,
    The Secret of the Stolen Signals.

GARRY GRAYSON SHOWING HIS SPEED; or,
    A Daring Run on the Gridiron.

GARRY GRAYSON AT STANLEY PREP; or, The
    Football Rivals of Riverview.

GROSSET & DUNLAP, *Publishers*, NEW YORK

THE RADIO BOYS SERIES

(Trademark Registered)

By ALLEN CHAPMAN

Author of the "Railroad Series," Etc.

**Individual Colored Wrappers. Illustrated.
Every Volume Complete in Itself.**

A new series for boys giving full details of radio work, both in sending and receiving—telling how small and large amateur sets can be made and operated, and how some boys got a lot of fun and adventure out of what they did. Each volume from first to last is so thoroughly fascinating, so strictly up-to-date and accurate, we feel sure all lads will peruse them with great delight.

Each volume has a Foreword by Jack Binns, the well-known radio expert.

GROSSET & DUNLAP, *Publishers,* NEW YORK

THE DON STURDY SERIES
By VICTOR APPLETON

**Individual Colored Wrappers and Text Illustrations by
WALTER S. ROGERS
Every Volume Complete in Itself.**

In company with his uncles, one a mighty hunter and the other a noted scientist, Don Sturdy travels far and wide, gaining much useful knowledge and meeting many thrilling adventures.

DON STURDY ON THE DESERT OF MYSTERY;
An engrossing tale of the Sahara Desert, of encounters with wild animals and crafty Arabs.

DON STURDY WITH THE BIG SNAKE HUNTERS;
Don's uncle, the hunter, took an order for some of the biggest snakes to be found in South America—to be delivered alive!

DON STURDY IN THE TOMBS OF GOLD;
A fascinating tale of exploration and adventure in the Valley of Kings in Egypt.

DON STURDY ACROSS THE NORTH POLE;
A great polar blizzard nearly wrecks the airship of the explorers.

DON STURDY IN THE LAND OF VOLCANOES;
An absorbing tale of adventures among the volcanoes of Alaska.

DON STURDY IN THE PORT OF LOST SHIPS;
This story is just full of exciting and fearful experiences on the sea.

DON STURDY AMONG THE GORILLAS;
A thrilling story of adventure in darkest Africa. Don is carried over a mighty waterfall into the heart of gorilla land.

GROSSET & DUNLAP, *Publishers,* NEW YORK

THE TOM SWIFT SERIES
By VICTOR APPLETON

Uniform Style of Binding. Individual Colored Wrappers. Every Volume Complete in Itself.

Every boy possesses some form of inventive genius. Tom Swift is a bright, ingenious boy and his inventions and adventures make the most interesting kind of reading.

TOM SWIFT AND HIS MOTOR CYCLE
TOM SWIFT AND HIS MOTOR BOAT
TOM SWIFT AND HIS AIRSHIP
TOM SWIFT AND HIS SUBMARINE BOAT
TOM SWIFT AND HIS ELECTRIC RUNABOUT
TOM SWIFT AND HIS WIRELESS MESSAGE
TOM SWIFT AMONG THE DIAMOND MAKERS
TOM SWIFT IN THE CAVES OF ICE
TOM SWIFT AND HIS SKY RACER
TOM SWIFT AND HIS ELECTRIC RIFLE
TOM SWIFT IN THE CITY OF GOLD
TOM SWIFT AND HIS AIR GLIDER
TOM SWIFT IN CAPTIVITY
TOM SWIFT AND HIS WIZARD CAMERA
TOM SWIFT AND HIS GREAT SEARCHLIGHT
TOM SWIFT AND HIS GIANT CANNON
TOM SWIFT AND HIS PHOTO TELEPHONE
TOM SWIFT AND HIS AERIAL WARSHIP
TOM SWIFT AND HIS BIG TUNNEL
TOM SWIFT IN THE LAND OF WONDERS
TOM SWIFT AND HIS WAR TANK
TOM SWIFT AND HIS AIR SCOUT
TOM SWIFT AND HIS UNDERSEA SEARCH
TOM SWIFT AMONG THE FIRE FIGHTERS
TOM SWIFT AND HIS ELECTRIC LOCOMOTIVE
TOM SWIFT AND HIS FLYING BOAT
TOM SWIFT AND HIS GREAT OIL GUSHER
TOM SWIFT AND HIS CHEST OF SECRETS
TOM SWIFT AND HIS AIRLINE EXPRESS

GROSSET & DUNLAP, PUBLISHERS, NEW YORK